Memories flooded her...

She remembered that voice. Her gaze shot toward the sound, and there he stood. Ronin. His voice had triggered the memories of that fateful night she was almost killed like her father.

"It was your father who rescued me, wasn't it?"

He nodded as he pulled her close. "It will be okay."

"That's what he said. That it would all be all right. And look at us. Does this look okay?" They were trapped in a snowstorm in a strange house in the middle of nowhere.

Ronin wanted to make the memories less painful for her and somehow help her arrange the jumbled pieces.

He should be happy. That was what he wanted after all. For her to remember. She was the only person, other than the true murderer, who could prove his father's innocence.

"Bringing me home helps clear his name." She looked into his eyes. "Is that the real reason you saved me? Not for *me*?"

He was saved from answering as the lights went out.

Tammy Johnson grew up as a preacher's kid. Her childhood was filled with moving and imaginary friends. She loves writing strong, independent heroines with strength of faith and character and heroes of equal convictions and charisma. She lives in a small Kansas town with her teenage son and dachshund. She enjoys cloud-watching and summer storms. A glass of sweet tea and a new story are never far away.

Books by Tammy Johnson

Love Inspired Suspense

Royal Rescue

ROYAL RESCUE

TAMMY JOHNSON

HARLEQUIN® LOVE INSPIRED® SUSPENSE

Recycling programs
for this product may
not exist in your area.

 LOVE INSPIRED BOOKS

ISBN-13: 978-0-373-67674-3

Royal Rescue

Copyright © 2015 by Tammy Johnson

www.Harlequin.com

Printed in U.S.A.

And I will be a Father unto you, and
ye shall be my sons and daughters, saith the Lord Almighty.
–2 Corinthians 6:18

To my children — You were my first dream come true. Without you, I might never have learned how strong I could be or how much I was capable of loving and being loved.

Tiffany — May you never settle. Someday your prince will come, until then be your own princess.

Nickolas — Thank you for helping me stay on task with my writing. I will always treasure our nights of writing together.

Mason — I have always admired your passion for life. Always ask the questions. Someday you will find your answers.

Kody — Maybe you can't be a superhero, but you will always have the heart of a protector. Stay strong and courageous.

No matter where your lives lead, I will always be proud of each of you and I will always love you.

God — thank You for the words. Thank You for this blessing. Thank You for being Love and showing me a little every day what real Love means.

Acknowledgments

Thank you to my amazing editor, Shana Asaro, who believed in me and picked me for her team during the Killer Voices pitch event. I hope this is only the beginning of great things.

Thank you to my brother for the sermon that got me back into writing, and to my sister, mother and family for never giving up on me. Thank you to Kimmi for the monthly phone calls over the years asking if I was writing.

ONE

It was easy to get lost in a crowd. Years of hiding had taught her that.

Thea James had gotten quite good at it, too. Her life had become a montage of staying one step ahead, never remaining in one place very long, keeping people at arm's length. That was the part she disliked the most—never getting too close.

Two things had gotten her through the past fourteen years of loneliness. The first and most important was her faith. The other was this day.

Her brother, Leo, was to meet her here. Meeting once a year was the one risk they took that neither could go without, and this remote Missouri city was a central location for both of them.

She checked her watch, hoping it would show she was early. They always timed it just right—5:00 p.m. in front of the courthouse.

Surrounded by people all in a hurry to get home to warm houses and home-cooked meals, they could go unnoticed. For a few blissful, irreplaceable moments they could be themselves once again.

Thea adjusted the ball cap on her head, making sure her hair was still tucked up neatly beneath its worn edges. She pulled her oversize winter coat tighter and glanced around, searching for the matching cap her brother said he'd wear so she could spot him more easily. A gust of freezing wind blew against her. The icy chill in the air reached through her skin, grabbing her heart.

People bustled around her. Most of them had their heads down, scarves draped in front of their faces to protect against the biting wind. No one gave her a first glance, let alone a second, but still she sensed it.

Something was wrong.

Her fingers tightened around the medallion in her pocket. The raised family crest on its surface had nearly worn smooth from the many times she'd rubbed her fingers over it. It was all she had left of her family. Her past life faded away more and more every day into something that felt less like a memory and more like a dream. Ever since the attack at the safe house last week she'd been on edge.

Every loud noise reminded her of gunfire, and every stranger was someone who might mean her harm.

But this was more than nerves.

She took a deep breath and whispered a quick prayer for strength.

The hair spiked on the back of her neck as a voice spoke behind her.

"Come with me." The words were spoken so low for a brief moment she thought she'd imagined them, that the wind had merely carried a memory to her. A firm hand grasped her elbow and she jerked around to face a man wearing a red cap identical to hers. But he was neither a memory nor her brother.

Her eyes darted around her, checking the escape route she'd planned earlier.

"That's not a good idea." He spoke as if sensing her intent to run. His voice was soft and steady with a warm whisper of empathy. "You really don't want to attract attention. Do you?"

Thea glanced up into the brightest blue eyes she'd ever seen. An eyebrow arched as he studied her, waiting for a reply. Deep in his eyes she saw a hint of compassion. But if she'd learned nothing else these past few years, she'd learned compassion could be faked. He was right in thinking she didn't want to make a scene, but if he thought she'd just stand here and meekly do as he asked, he thought wrong.

"The way I see it, you are far more likely to gain attention if you try to stop me," she said.

His grip tightened on her arm. Her eyes flew to his fingers—long and manly, they held her with a firm, confident grip.

"Maybe, but do you really want to put your theory to the test?" He tugged her against him as he spoke. Even through the layers of his heavy winter coat, she could feel his strength, sense his controlled power.

Her mind raced with options. She could scream. She could take the chance that somewhere in the hustle of the few people still leaving the building there would be one Good Samaritan who would come to her aid. There was a chance she'd be able to slip away unnoticed during the rescue attempt. There was also a chance she wouldn't. Judging by the determined look deep in his steely blue eyes, he wouldn't give up easily. Any do-gooder from the small town wouldn't stand much of a chance against him.

"I could scream and have a police officer here within minutes."

Despite the bluster of her words and thoughts, she stood frozen in compliance. Obedience had for such a long time been her first instinct. Everyone had always told her where to go, when to be still, when to run. She was good at running. But she was tired.

"That would be foolish and waste time." He held her tightly against him, barely giving her space to breathe. "Time is something we don't have an abundance of right now. Trust me. I'm here to help you."

Part of her wanted to believe him, but she didn't.

"I don't need help." She was here to meet her brother, not this man. She raised her chin and met his gaze. It had taken her a few years to discover she had a backbone. It had taken even longer to learn how to use it. "Especially not the sort of help that involves grabbing me and nearly yanking my arm off."

"I can't help you if you run. If I let go of your arm, we both know that's what you'll do."

"You must have me confused with someone else." The alarm bells that had been going off in her head resounded even louder. "As I said, I don't need your help." Slowly she jiggled her shoulder just enough to let the weight of her bag slide the strap down her arm.

"Whether you realize it or not, you do. You need to come with me." His unwavering gaze steadied on her and she stiffened, worried he sensed her intent. "Now," he added in a firm tone, his breath a cloud of frosty, minty air between them.

"What I need is for you to let go of me." She tugged against his hold on her arm.

His grip held firm.

"You are Princess Dorthea Elizabeth Jamison, aren't you?"

A prickle of unease raced up her spine. He knew who she was. In the past that had rarely been a good thing.

When she didn't deny or confirm his question, he continued.

"My name is Ronin Parrish. Your brother sent me." He took his eyes off her for a second, skimming their surroundings as if looking for something or someone. "We need to go. We've already stayed here longer than we should have."

Fear swept through her. Her brother wasn't coming.

Leo would never have stayed away willingly, and he would never have given up her location, despite what this man might say. After all these years, the people who had killed her father had finally come after her, killing her bodyguard in the process. They must have gone after Leo, as well. Whoever this man was, he knew far more than he should. The fact that he was here and not her brother could mean he had a part in keeping him away.

It could also mean he was telling the truth. But that was not a risk she was willing to take. She shook the thoughts of her brother away and dug deep for the strength she knew God had given her. She would have time later to deal with the emotions flooding her as she considered what might have happened to him. Every second she wasted ticked away at the time she had to find a safe place to think what her next step should be.

Self-preservation kicked in.

She grabbed the straps of her shoulder bag tightly in her hand and swung it with all her might toward his head. It made contact with a thud. He lost his footing, falling to one knee. His grip on her arm loosened. With a quick tug, she wrenched her arm away and ran.

She could hear him stumbling and then his feet crunching in the snow as he regained his balance. The sound grew more distant as she ran. She didn't slow. She didn't dare risk the time it would take to look over her shoulder to see how much of a lead she had.

Fear spurred her on. Her feet slipped on the icy sidewalk. If the chase continued out in the open he'd catch her easily. His legs were longer and he was doubtless well trained. He'd catch her, then he'd kill her.

The thought gave her a burst of speed. She'd shown up tonight with her escape plan in place. She'd learned from those who had protected her how important a quick getaway could be, and along the way she'd picked up a few tricks of her own.

She ducked between the evergreen bushes that lined the pathway separating the park and the courthouse. Hugging the stone wall as close as possible, she dropped the bright red baseball cap to the snow-covered ground and replaced it with a darker, woolen stocking cap from her pocket. Hopefully, the quick change would keep her from standing out. She turned the corner at the end of the block and darted between cars parked along the street. Carefully she weaved in and out of the few people on the sidewalk and slid into the diner on the corner.

The smell of fried foods hit her with the blast of warm air. Her stomach growled, reminding her of how long it had been since her last real meal. A quick glance out the large picture window showed no sign of the man, but he couldn't be far behind.

She breathed a sigh of relief. She would be safe now. The small room was nearly filled with people. Elderly men sat along the fifties-style bar with steaming mugs in front of them. Thea dashed past booths of vinyl and Formica occupied by couples and families and headed to the women's restroom at the back.

She was fairly certain he wouldn't try to break in the bathroom door in front of everyone in the small diner. Once inside she locked the door and leaned against it just long enough to take a deep breath. More likely than not, if he followed her to the diner, he'd sit outside waiting for her. As if she would have a change of heart and just walk out and docilely do as he said.

He seemed the sort who was accustomed to people doing what he told them to do.

The tiny niggling of doubt flared its ugly head again. He really could be here to help her. She dismissed it. It didn't matter. Many people had died trying to help her. She'd made a decision after what had happened last week at the safe house. The memory of those who had died trying to protect her would be something she carried with her forever. She would not be the cause of any more death. She had a chance to escape and she was going to take it.

The window above the toilet was the gateway to her future. It looked barely large enough for her to get through. The toilet bowl had no cover and the lid on the tank looked wobbly at best, but it was the window and freedom or the man and whatever plans he might have.

The strong odor of disinfectant assailed her as she stepped up onto the seat, balancing a foot on each side. Maneuvering onto the tank, she grabbed the windowsill as her support wobbled. Thea overadjusted and lost her precarious footing on the tank. Her chin came down hard on the ledge and she just managed to keep a foot from slipping into the bowl. But she was okay.

A few hard pushes on the window loosened the old paint enough to get it open, and she once again climbed up onto the tank. Knowing it would be a tight squeeze, she took off her jacket and dropped it and her bag through the window to the ground outside. She threw first one leg, then the other over the ledge and squirmed feetfirst through the small opening.

"Couldn't get out the normal way?" a familiar male voice inquired from just behind her.

A flush coursed through her body as she realized the view she must be giving him, and she shimmied frantically to dislodge herself from her position. A sharp stinging sensation shot up her leg at the same time as the sound of tearing material. The more she pushed, the more it dug into her skin and the more her jeans ripped.

"I think you're stuck on something."

Thea snorted, a very unladylike sound.

She was at his mercy. His hands grasped her hips and pulled. After a few tugs and a little more wiggling, she was free. He lifted her body with ease. As little as she wanted to admit it, he was strong. Even stronger than she'd first imagined. The feel of him holding her briefly took her back to a place where she'd felt safe. It would be so easy to relax against him and let him protect her. Just as quickly the thought was gone and she was reminded that his strength was also a means to easily over-power her if he chose to. As her feet touched the ground, she turned to face him.

The humor that had been barely noticeable in his voice hadn't yet reached his face; if any-thing he appeared more dangerous than he had before.

"Ever heard of a door?"

"In case you hadn't noticed, I was attempt-ing to give you the slip," she said as she picked up her jacket from the ground.

"And how's that working out for you?" This time she detected a soft hint of laughter in his voice.

"I think that's painfully obvious."

"It is, isn't it?" he said, his lips tilting into a crooked grin. Then he turned and motioned with a swing of his arm for her to walk in front of him. "But hopefully, now you are ready to come with me."

She ignored his motion and faced him, toe to toe.

"If you are here to kill me, just do it." She quickly pushed her arms into her jacket and wrapped it tightly around her. "But don't expect me to make it any easier for you."

"I'm not here to kill you, Princess Dorthea." He reached for her bag on the ground near his feet. He held it out between them, testing its weight and eyeing her suspiciously. "Are you carrying around the kitchen sink?"

"It's a brick." She grabbed for her bag, but he held it just out of her reach while removing her only means of protection. He then handed it back over to her.

"You won't need the brick anymore. As I've already said, I'm here to rescue you."

She snorted again. "Some rescue. I'm freezing and I've banged my chin." She motioned where it had slammed against the windowsill. "I've ripped my jeans and who knows if I've torn skin, as well. If you were any good at your job, you could make my death quicker instead of slowly bruising me to death."

He smiled and for the first time she really took the time to notice him as a man. Not just as a danger she needed to avoid. He was quite handsome in a rugged and ruthless sort of way.

"You are very right. If I were going to kill you, I'd have done it in a much more humane manner and much more quickly. I'd probably have shot you when you hit me in the head with your brick-loaded bag. Or perhaps a poison apple would be more your style?"

A lock of dark blond bangs fell across his forehead. Combined with the smile, it gave him a mischievous look. For a slight moment her heart warmed toward him. As a bitter north wind blew, bits of sleet began to pelt them, stinging her exposed skin before melting against her warmth.

Thea held herself in check to keep from smiling back at him. She felt a stab of guilt at the swollen gash on his forehead. A thin trickle of dried blood stained the side of his face. She shook off the feeling. There was still a chance, however small, that he meant to harm her.

"Let's just pretend for a moment I might believe you." She slung the strap of her bag over her shoulder and looked up into his eyes. "Why are you here? What has happened to my brother? And don't give me that 'I'm here to rescue you' line again. I want the truth."

"I will always be truthful with you, Princess. As I told you before, my name is Ronin

Parrish. Your brother sent me to find you and keep you safe. You are in grave danger."

Her heart lurched in her chest. The name was familiar, but she didn't have time to place how she knew it. Her brother was her focus. Leo wouldn't send someone to her unless something was terribly wrong. Images of him suffering, lying near death or worse, flooded her mind. She closed her eyes and prayed for the gut-wrenching fear to be replaced with peace. She prayed for her brother and that he would have the same peace and strength to get through whatever had happened to keep him away.

"My brother wouldn't send someone unless it wasn't possible for him to come on his own." Confusion flooded her. She needed Leo. More so this year than any of the others they'd met here. "Is he…?" She couldn't bear to finish the sentence or the thought.

"No." The simple word sent a flood of relief and thankfulness through her. Ronin reached for her, but she pulled away. "I'm here to bring you home."

"Home?" The word was a mere whisper on her lips. She hadn't set foot in her country of Portase in fourteen years. All she had left of her home were the memories that had grown more and more unclear with time. At first she'd dreamed of the day she could return, but as the years had passed, thoughts of home had brought only fear. "I can never go home."

As badly as she still wanted to, a part of her was afraid to accept it. So many happy memories had been buried beneath the ash that had once meant everything to her. Quickly on the heels were the bad memories, the knowledge that someone there wanted to see her dead.

"You still haven't answered my question." He'd done a fine job of dancing around it. His evasiveness did nothing to ease her suspicion of him. "Tell me. What has happened to my brother?"

Thea held her breath waiting for the answer she needed to hear even though she was certain she wouldn't like it.

"He's been shot."

Ronin Parrish had anticipated a few different scenarios of his first meeting with Princess Dorthea. In all of them he'd save the day and she'd come along with him with very little argument. He hadn't expected the woman standing in front of him, who looked as if she wasn't sure whether to run or pummel him again with her bag.

At least he'd had the foresight to remove the brick from it if she did.

"Shot?" She choked the single word out on a fragile whisper.

The pain he heard in her voice made him want to take her in his arms and tell her everything was going to be okay. But he couldn't. Not only would she not let him within two feet of her without running, but he wasn't convinced himself. He was many things, but he wasn't a liar. He wouldn't sugarcoat the situation just to gain her cooperation.

"He's in the hospital, but his condition is stable and the doctors expect a full recovery."

"Take me to him." Her words sounded very much like a command, but there was a slight waver in her voice. She was strong. Much stronger than he'd imagined. That characteristic could be both good and bad all wrapped up in one tiny princess package.

"I can't do that." Having both the royal heirs in the same place at the same time now would only lead to disaster. Every means possible must be used to keep them apart until the threat against them was identified and eliminated.

"I don't believe you." Suspicion lit her mossy-green eyes and she shuffled backward. "How do I know you aren't the one who shot him?"

She was still afraid of him. Not that he could

blame her. It would be difficult to trust after the pain and suffering she'd already endured in her twenty-four years. Her mother had died years before, during the birth of her younger sister. Her sister had only been three years old when their father, the king, had been killed, and she'd been lost in the fire that had been set in an attempt to cover his murder.

Leo was all she had left. Being separated from him these past fourteen years had probably taken its toll on her. The next few weeks wouldn't be any easier than what she had already faced, but there was too much at stake to risk losing her now.

"I didn't shoot your brother." Even to him the words seemed like too little. He could only hope she would believe the sincerity in his voice. Now that he finally had the truth within his grasp, he would not let it go.

She was thinking of running again. He could sense it. Feel it as tangibly as the tiny shards of frozen rain beating against his skin. Ronin took a deep breath and squelched the urge to step toward her. Her eyes widened with apprehension. She was ready to flee. He knew she would run until there was no strength left in her. Her instincts were on target. She was in danger.

But not from him.

She took a larger step away, then another.

His mind raced. He could grab her and haul her to his car. There would be kicking and screaming involved. Not exactly the best way to go about gaining her confidence. Short of knocking her unconscious, which was really not an option, he had one shot at swaying her over to willingness.

"There is only one way you are ever going to see your brother again." He hated using her brother and her need to see him as bribery. But it was the truth. Whether she knew it or not, she really only had one option.

Him. He just had to convince her of that.

She stopped in her tracks but made no move to step in his direction.

Her stillness gave him hope.

Icy pellets crunched beneath his feet as he took a small step toward her.

A gust of bitter wind blew wisps of hair free from her cap. Russet strands danced across her face but didn't hide the uncertainty that swept over her features. He couldn't blame her for not trusting him. A tiny part of him admired the way she followed her instincts.

"And what way is that?" Her voice was a soft whisper. Gone was all the gusto she'd tossed at him mere moments ago.

"Come with me."

"You must think I'm a fool."

Ronin thought her many things, but a fool was not one of them. She was one of the only people alive who could tell the truth of what had happened the night her father, the king, had been killed. Since that night she'd not spoken of what she'd seen or heard. The secrets buried somewhere in her mind made her an even bigger target than her brother. Not only was she heir to the throne as the firstborn, but she also held the power to condemn the real person responsible for the king's death. The wrong man had been imprisoned. Ronin knew that to be absolute.

She held the knowledge that could free his father.

"Come with me and you'll see your brother again. Arrangements are being made this moment for you to reclaim the throne that was taken from your father."

"That is lunacy."

"Is it?" he asked.

"Why now?" She stared at him. Her face was nearly devoid of any emotion. Her lips parted, then closed. An argument of pros and cons seemed to war behind her questioning eyes. He could only hope he was close to gaining her cooperation. "We were safe before last week. What has changed to make someone come after me after all this time?"

So many things, he thought. He was unsure of where to begin.

A car passed by them on the street, reminding him of their surroundings. The streetlights crackled and flickered to life just beyond where she stood near the curb. The icy snow mixture was falling heavier, and it was getting darker. He'd hoped to be on the road before night fell.

"Princess Dorthea, there is a lot to explain. But not here."

She needed to know the truth. She deserved it. He would not keep that from her. He had nothing to hide. He was finished hiding. When he had been sent to bring Leo in, it had taken weeks to gain his trust. Once he had, they had become close friends and Leo had shown him the peace that could only come from living completely in the truth.

Leo had believed in him even when their country hadn't.

A few seconds ticked away, but it felt like minutes. He didn't have the benefit of weeks like he'd had with the prince. He watched her, the play of emotions sweeping over her face. She chewed at her bottom lip, her uncertain eyes glancing around her, then back at him. He noticed the instant she made her decision.

At that same moment he spotted the car at the end of the block, its bright lights beamed in their direction. Its tires spun in the ice and gravel mixture covering the road, sending an eerie squeal through the night as it headed toward them.

Toward her.

TWO

Thea gasped as the car's wheels spun on the snow-slicked pavement. The driver revved the engine and the car made a beeline for her. Her first instinct was to say a quick prayer as she waited for it to slow or turn. Instead, it picked up speed.

A quick glance at the man she'd distanced herself from showed he'd noticed the car, as well. His gaze darted between her and the vehicle. This wasn't the first time she'd faced death. Like the other times, someone was with her. The fact that she wouldn't be facing it alone should give her some solace.

It didn't.

Out of the corner of her eye she could see Ronin rushing toward her. He would die for her. If anything, knowing he would try to save her made her even more terrified.

On instinct, she turned to run, too, to save herself, but her feet slipped out from under her and she hit the pavement. The ground was frozen and slick beneath her as she turned, hoping to get to her feet. But before she could, she was pulled against a hard body. Ronin's strong arms encircled her, encasing her in a cocoon of safety.

His warmth seemed so familiar yet so new all at the same time. The fuzzy memory was so close she could almost reach out and pluck it from her mind. Just as quickly as it came, it was gone.

He rolled against the pavement, pulling her with him. Thea buried her face against him. They landed in a heap of tangled arms and legs against the far curb. The car flew by in a whoosh of air, barely missing them.

Ronin held her close, but she turned her head against his chest to see the car attempt to screech to a stop after passing them by. The sudden braking sent the car spinning out of control on the ice. Metal scraped metal as the car sideswiped the few vehicles parked in front of the diner.

"Are you hurt?" Ronin asked, sitting them upright. He quickly ran his hands over her arms and legs, checking for broken bones.

"I'm not sure." Thea closed her eyes tightly, then opened them slowly in an attempt to clear her head. Her body shook with the gamut of emotions flooding her. She was alive and thankful for that.

The car continued its slide down the street. It came to a stop only when its front fender smashed into a light pole at the far end of the street. Sirens sounded in the distance.

"Can you stand?" His voice was filled with concern as he stood, then outstretched his hand to help her to her feet. Two black-clad figures stumbled from the vehicle. Thea watched in shock as they pointed in her direction. They were men, big and bulky, about the same height as Ronin. One of them reached inside his coat and pulled out a handgun, waving it in her direction as the other man shouted and made wild gestures with his hands.

The sirens grew louder. Blue and red police lights lit the night sky.

"Can you stand?" Ronin repeated, louder this time as he grabbed her hand. He pulled her to her feet without waiting for an answer. "We need to go, Princess."

Thea gave no protest as he wrapped his arm around her shoulders. It was only a matter of time before the men finished whatever argument they were having and came after them. Worse yet, they might decide to use their guns and start shooting at them. She followed Ronin's lead as he guided her across the city square and the park to where he'd left his car. Sleek and black, it was exactly what she would expect him to drive. Dangerous yet powerful, just like the man who controlled it. He held the door open for her, but before giving in to the compliance she knew was expected of her, she risked one last, quick glance around her.

Police sirens grew closer. He was right. They had to go. Staying would endanger not only them, but also any innocent bystanders who might get in the way if the men came after them. The local police would be here soon, but men like these held no regard for the police. She slid into the passenger seat, her body strangely numb to everything going on around her. She barely noticed as Ronin grabbed her seat belt and fastened it across her.

Within moments they were leaving the small town behind them.

Tiny bits of ice hit the windshield, the wipers keeping a steady rhythm in an attempt to keep the windshield clear.

"They were trying to kill me."

She glanced over at Ronin in the driver's seat. His eyes remained on the road ahead, except for occasional glances in the rearview mirror.

He had risked his life for her.

"We could have both been killed," she whispered.

"You're safe now, Princess Dorthea." She knew his words meant to calm her, but safe was something she hadn't felt for a very long time.

Part of her was still wary of him, but the way she'd felt when he'd wrapped his arm over her shoulder and steered her to the car had sent her back in time. It had brought back the memories of when another man, much older, had protected her and made her feel safe when her world had been falling apart. For so long she'd hoped and prayed for a life that was normal again. Safe would be nice.

"Thea," she said. "My name is Thea now."

She wasn't sure if he was even listening now, but she cringed every time he used her formal name. Princess Dorthea was a person people died for. She was tired of that person. It might be her title, but she wasn't a princess anymore. She wasn't sure if she ever really wanted to be again.

Thea relaxed against the headrest and took a deep breath. Her stomach turned, both from hunger and the stress of the events of the evening. She fought against the nausea rising in her throat. Asking him to pull over so she could vomit was one humiliation she'd prefer to not have to deal with.

In an attempt to take her mind off her stomach, she turned her head to study Ronin's profile. Thea couldn't quite put her finger on what was so familiar about him. Maybe he looked like someone she'd once seen in a movie or on television years ago. That must be it. He just had that sort of face.

"Is everything okay?" he asked, catching her staring at him.

"That's a silly question." Thea attempted a laugh, but it emerged as more of a choked squeak.

"Yeah, I guess so."

"I'm sorry about your head and the brick." Thea reached toward his face, her fingertips brushing over the nasty cut just above his eyebrow.

"Are you?" he questioned.

"Yes, I am. Despite my earlier behavior, I'm not the sort of person who runs around bashing unsuspecting men upside the head."

"If it makes you feel any better, I wasn't totally unsuspecting."

She smiled at his remark.

"And if it makes *you* feel any better, it probably won't scar."

"Even if it did, it would blend right in with the few I have already."

"Well, then it would make you look even more dangerous." Thea studied his face, taking in the few faint lines of small scars she'd not noticed earlier. He'd seen his fair share of battles of one sort or another. "I assume looking dangerous comes in handy in your line of work."

"And what sort of work is it that you think I am in, exactly?"

"I think it's safe to say you would have killed me by now if that was your intent. So you must really be here to rescue me."

Thea wasn't sure exactly what job title that would be. It really didn't matter. Given her true identity and the circumstances under which they'd met, she assumed it would be safe to say he was a bodyguard in some shape or form. If he'd been anything less, she imagined the brick would have sent him running.

"You're going to have quite the bruise yourself." He nodded toward her chin.

"That was my own doing, though. I'm a bit clumsy when it comes to balancing on wobbly toilet tanks."

"Are you hurt anywhere else?"

"Everything seems to be in working order." Thea stretched her legs and wiggled her arms around as proof. She felt a twinge of pain, but bruising was expected after the ordeal they'd been through.

"Still, as soon as I'm sure we're not being followed, we'll find a spot to pull over and stretch our legs just to be sure. Maybe pick up some food, too."

Her stomach turned again. It had been days since she'd eaten.

"I'd like that." She glanced over at him. He knew her name, but how much more did he know? "I have no money," she added. When the safe house where she'd lived for the past year had been overrun, she'd barely had time to grab her bag. Her guards had told her to run and she'd run. Just like a good little princess.

"I know," he replied in a gentle tone. "You must be starving."

"I am hungry."

The few dollars she had saved from her part-time job at the local diner had lasted only a couple days. She'd slept where she could find a safe spot and survived on vending-machine snacks, just getting by, waiting for today, when she was supposed to meet Leo.

Leo would have known what to do.

She had complete trust in her brother, and he'd sent this man to her. She sneaked a glance at his strong profile again. For the time being she would have to trust him, too. There was something about him that still raised warning flags in her mind. He had secrets, things he hadn't shared completely with her. But she'd see this through. Despite her reservations about going home, she needed her brother. If this man could take her to him, then she'd go along with him for now. But that didn't mean she'd trust him blindly.

Something about him and this situation didn't sit quite right, but she would find a way to turn it around, even if it meant letting him be her protector for a few days. It would be worth it to see her brother. If there was even a remote chance she could be reunited with Leo, she would take it. For so many years she'd only dreamed of having a normal life once again. It wasn't easy to trust him, but what choice did she have?

She didn't like needing someone else to fight her battles for her, and she didn't want to endanger any other lives. But she was smart enough to know she'd never find the answers without help. He was her best chance at finally finding out who had killed her father and wanted her dead. Once that person was caught and punished, she'd at least have a chance at a normal family once again.

* * *

She attacked the plate of french fries as if she hadn't eaten in weeks. As soon as the waitress had placed the meal in front of her, Thea had bowed her head and given a quiet prayer of thanks, then dug into the food with her full attention.

A twinge of guilt shot through him. He'd driven longer than he probably needed to, but he couldn't take the chance they were being followed. Even now they were taking a chance. But she had to eat.

There was a very real possibility this was the first meal she'd had in days. Her most recent safe house had been compromised last week. Ronin hated to think of how she'd been surviving since. Or how she'd even managed to make it out safely. He smiled to himself. She probably went out through a window. Not that it was a laughing matter. She was in very real danger. He'd do well to not let himself get too comfortable with her. He needed to keep reminding himself of that.

Her safety had to come first.

He checked his watch. They'd driven for several hours. It would be midnight soon. With the weather it had been slow going. It didn't help that he'd stuck to using mostly back roads.

There had been no sign of any other vehicles in miles, besides those whose drivers had lost control and ended up in ditches along the highway. Like he'd promised, when he was sure they were safe, he'd pulled over for a much needed break and food.

They sat at a table near the back of the truck stop. Only a few people—all truckers from what he could tell—were out at this time of night and in these conditions. From his position he had a good view of the entrance over Thea's shoulder. Ronin took a bite of his fries, hoping she wouldn't notice how intently he'd been watching her and the doorway behind her. She'd been on edge since they'd left the town behind them. Not that he could blame her. The fact that she hadn't fainted dead away or lapsed into a fit of hysteria spoke a great deal for her inner strength.

He'd studied every written fact about the princess for months knowing that she was probably the best, if not only, hope he had of clearing his father's name. But all of the studying he'd done hadn't begun to prepare him for the truth of who she really was. All of the words written on paper couldn't really capture the essence of her.

Although after all this time and all she'd been through he hadn't expected a pampered, tiara-wearing princess. He watched her take a very large, unladylike bite of her cheeseburger. He hadn't really anticipated her being able to blend into her surroundings so well, either. He should have known better. "Expect the unexpected" was a good motto to live by.

Despite the fact she had learned her fair share of survival techniques, he could still see a softness around the edges. She would be offended to know he noticed.

By all appearances she was paying him little attention while she ate her meal. But he'd caught her watching him, even though she'd kept her eyes lowered. She was guarded and wary. Both were good qualities to have when you weren't sure where danger might be lurking. She'd be wise to not trust every stranger they might come across.

She was wise to not trust him.

"You have some ketchup…" He made a motion at the corner of his own mouth, hoping she'd find the spot. "Right there."

The tip of her tongue flicked around the corner of her mouth, licking her pink lips clean.

"It's not polite to stare."

"I'm sorry, Princess Dorthea." When she shot him a glare, he corrected himself. "Thea."

"You must think I've turned into a barbarian." A juicy hamburger grease mixture with mayo and tomato ran down her fingers. She set the remainder on her plate and used her napkin to wipe her hands clean.

"If I were going to think you barbaric, it would have been when you hit me with that brick."

"I might do it again if I felt threatened." She smiled but he knew how serious she was. He could already tell she was very stubborn. That was just another characteristic about her that surprised him.

"No matter how sorry it made you, of course," he teased, tossing back her earlier statement.

"Of course," she agreed with a nervous laugh.

"While I admire that you are capable of taking care of yourself, your brick-wielding days are over. I'm here to protect you now."

He heard her sharp intake of breath and noticed the flash of daring in her eyes but was spared the reply as the waitress walked up to their table.

"Can I get you guys a refill?"

"Yes, please." Thea pushed her nearly empty glass of water to the edge of the table, where the waitress could pour from the pitcher she held in her hand.

Ronin nodded and did the same.

"I hope you're planning on leaving a good tip," Thea said after the waitress had walked away. "Most waitresses live on tips, you know."

He couldn't say that he knew or didn't. It was one of those things that in this place and time didn't really matter much in the grand scheme of things. But it mattered to her.

Thea fidgeted with the straw in her drink, swirling it around between the ice cubes, staring at it, but he could tell her mind was somewhere else.

Ronin knew nearly everything there was to know about her. She'd been allowed to work part-time as a waitress at local diners near her last few homes. The choice had been a foolish one. Being in the open made her an easy target. If not for the fact any money the sympathizers had managed to get from the sale of family jewels and salvaged belongings had long ago run out, it probably wouldn't have even been considered. Although he'd only known Thea for a short time, he could imagine she'd been very stubborn about wanting to pay her own way.

Foolish or not, the job might have saved her life.

"I worked as a waitress." Thea pulled her hands back and placed them in her lap. "I wasn't home when they came for me. A coworker asked me to cover a shift and I snuck out. I was at work. I came home and found them…" Her words trailed off.

Ronin reached across the table, willing her to take his hand so he could pull her from the terrifying memories she was lost in. Just then, the waitress reappeared, pad and pen out in front of her ready to tally up their meal and any extras she might be able to talk them into. "Can I get either of you some dessert?"

Thea jumped in her seat. For a brief moment he thought she might get up and run.

"I'm sorry, hon. Didn't mean to startle you," the waitress said, noticing Thea's edginess. "The pecan pie is very tasty and made fresh this afternoon. We even buy the pecans locally from a grove down the road."

"No nuts, thanks. We're allergic."

Thea eyed him from across the table. The fear seemed to change to suspicion.

"I think we're about finished up here," he said, glancing over at Thea. "Unless you would like something else?"

"I'm fine, thank you," Thea replied guardedly.

"Just the check, please," Ronin requested. The sooner they got back on the road, the better.

"Sure thing," the waitress replied. "You two aren't from around here, are you?"

"Just traveling through."

"We don't get many travelers this time of night, especially with this weather." She rambled as she totaled up their order, ripping the paper from the pad and laying it on the table next to his plate. "Now, in the summer, that's a different story. We have some of the best catfish fishing spots around just a few miles down the road."

Ronin pulled out a few bills, with a large tip figured in, and laid them on the table.

"I'll be right back with your change."

"You can keep it," Ronin replied.

"Thank you. That's mighty kind of you." She flashed him a big smile. "You two be careful out there. We don't usually get storms like this one this late in the year. Even so, it's turning into the worst storm in years. Many of the highways will be shut down soon if it keeps up."

"I'd like to use the restroom before we get back on the road," Thea stated after the waitress had gone.

Ronin wasn't sure if she was asking for permission or voicing a fact. The tone in her voice was one he hadn't heard from her yet. It left no room for argument. As she brushed past him, he couldn't help but wonder if he'd just been put in his place.

With large strides he caught up with her just before she entered the bathroom. Blocking the door, he flicked the light on and checked out the small room before letting her pass.

"I think we need to get something straight."

"We do?" Her eyebrows raised in question.

"Yes, we do." Ronin took a deep breath. "This is the way it's going to be. While I am protecting you, I am in charge." He paused, waiting for the argument he was sure would come before adding, "You will do as I say."

She crossed her arms in front of her and stared but said nothing. Was she mulling his words over in her mind or had she already totally dismissed them?

"You're not thinking of coming in here with me, are you?" she finally said.

"Not at all," he replied. He enjoyed the flash of fire in her eyes as he teased. "Just checking for windows."

Ronin leaned a shoulder against the wall by the door and waited. He might appear relaxed, but he kept his eyes and ears tuned to any movement and noise around them. That conversation had gone better than expected. There was a storm brewing in her mind, though. It was just a matter of time before she let it all loose on him.

He smiled. He rather enjoyed the idea of

that. He admired a woman who wouldn't just sit back and do as she was told. But the pluck had to be tempered with just the right amount of wisdom. There was a time and a place. He could only hope she fully understood now was the time to listen and do as she was asked.

Whether she liked it or not, he had to take the lead. His first priority was keeping her safe. He couldn't do that properly if she were questioning him at every turn or trying to run. The earlier attack proved how real the threat was. They had just been fortunate that the men hadn't used their guns earlier. He had seen one of the men pull his weapon. Then they'd argued. Probably about the police and the scene it would cause. But another attack was inevitable.

Now that rumors were circulating about the long-thought-dead prince and princess being alive and hidden away in the United States, there would be more attacks. They wouldn't stop.

If that information had stayed safely hidden away like it had for the past fourteen years, this would be a walk in the park. He would have stayed with Leo, and his brother Jarrod would have come for Thea. That had been their plan. But things hadn't gone according to plan. Leo had been shot, and more men had been sent to him. Then word had leaked about the prince and princess being alive. Ronin was the closest and had learned of her plan to meet her brother, so he'd come for Thea.

The person responsible for the information coming out early was just as guilty as the men who had attacked the safe house and killed innocent people. When the leak was found, he or she would be tried right along with the assassins.

He heard her shuffling around inside. He imagined her indignation at being watched over and told what to do. Like it or not, he would watch her a lot more closely now. When he was positive she was safe and sound at the royal estate just outside Denver, she could order him to take a very long hike if she wanted. But for now, she would do what he asked.

The door creaked open and she emerged. Without a word he helped her into her coat and they made their way outside. Only a few trucks and trailers were parked along the edges of the parking lot, and his car stood alone near the front. The wind blew with such force it was a struggle to walk a straight line. He wrapped his arm around Thea and together they trudged, heads down, to the car.

Out in the open and exposed as they were, his senses were on alert. If anyone were going to make a move, this would be the perfect time. Arriving at the car, he opened Thea's door and helped her inside before moving around to the driver's side. Quickly, he scraped off the snow and ice that had accumulated on the windshield before joining her inside. They might be safe now, but at any point another attempt could be made on Thea's life.

Despite the circumstances, he was actually looking forward to the long drive. She surprised him. In the short time he'd spent with her, he'd already begun to admire many things about her. One couldn't help but be drawn to her passion for life and caring spirit.

He glanced in her direction before pulling out onto the highway. Thea's eyes remained focused out her window. It was probably for the best. He needed to keep the distance he'd put between them by telling her the way things had to be. Getting too close and forgetting this was a job would jeopardize not only getting to the truth he craved, but also her life.

THREE

"How did you know about the nuts?" She'd been staring out the window, watching the snow fly by for the past hour or so. She was bored. Despite the fact she was annoyed with him, she couldn't sit and do nothing for another moment. Her mind had been so focused on his overbearing, macho orders, she'd nearly forgotten her curiosity over his remark about her allergy earlier.

Silence was her only immediate reply, and for a moment she wondered if she'd need to repeat herself or if he was going to answer at all.

"I know everything about you," he said quietly.

"Everything?" she asked. Surely he couldn't know everything. Her mind raced with some of the more private moments of her life that she wouldn't feel comfortable with a complete stranger knowing.

"You are a princess. Your life is well documented."

"Well documented?" Thea resisted the urge to shriek, but she felt it building inside her nonetheless. "Documented how?"

"Everything about you has been written down from the day you were born. Your first steps, your first smile. Your first tooth is on exhibit in a museum back home."

"Really?" she gasped, studying his profile.

"No." He glanced her way and shot her a quick smile. "I was only teasing about the tooth. But you have always been observed."

"You shouldn't tease me that way." Embarrassment coursed through her. She'd known she had always been watched and her family would forever be a part of their country's history. History was one thing, though. It was something to look back on years and years from now and ponder. They weren't things she wanted to share in the here and now. They definitely weren't things she wanted to share with a man who already thought he knew everything there was to know about her. It was unnerving that he quite possibly knew more about her than she remembered herself.

He smiled, a wide, knowing smile, and it only fueled her discomfort.

"It was important that I know all that I could

about you in order to do my job and properly protect you."

It was only a job. The fact should have lessened her embarrassment, but it didn't. It wasn't right that one person should know so much about another. It was an unfair advantage that he knew so much about her and she knew nothing about him.

"That's hardly fair." Thea crossed her arms and stared ahead out the windshield. The snow fell heavily in large, perfect flakes. It was as if they were in their own private spaceship on a voyage through the stars. Snowflakes zoomed by at what seemed like lightning speed, but she'd been watching the speedometer and knew they were barely crawling along at well below the speed limit. The beauty of the snow kept her mind from racing off through the many other things he might know about her that she'd rather he didn't.

"Would it make it fair if I told you something about me?"

"Of course it would." Any idea of who this man was would help if she were going to continue to hold her own against him. She had to have a clue of what she was up against.

"Then ask away."

She had no idea where to start. There were so many things that she wanted to know.

Jumbled thoughts of questions to ask ran through her mind.

"Do you believe in God?" In the dim light of the dashboard, she could see the play of emotions race across his face. It seemed she'd surprised him with her question. Her own faith and beliefs were central to her identity. She knew without a doubt she wouldn't be who she was now if her faith hadn't given her the strength to see the good that could come from all the bad she had experienced in her life. If she were going to trust him with her life and spend any amount of time with him, she needed to know if he shared her convictions.

"Yes," he answered.

Thea sensed there was a lot more he wasn't saying. For a moment she thought of pushing further but decided against it. He'd tell her more when he was ready, or she'd find out by his actions. Besides, there was much more she wanted to learn about the man who already knew her life story.

"Are you married?" As soon as the words were spoken, she wondered if she was being too nosey. "I'm sorry—it's none of my business."

"Don't be sorry. All's fair. After all, I'm fully aware that you are single. I could list the names, ages and social security numbers of the men you have seen socially, though, if you'd like." He chuckled and, although she knew he was teasing her, she rose to the challenge.

"You and I both know I've barely been allowed to make friends, let alone date." She paused for a moment. She wanted to make connections and have friends. But friendships were impossible when you were never allowed to stay in one place very long and were always being watched. "All right, then, I stand by my question." She'd noticed he wore no rings, although that didn't always mean a man was single. Not all men chose to wear rings.

"I'm single. Never married. I have dated, but nothing serious, really." He paused, flashing a grin. "Would you like names and ages?"

"I don't think that will be necessary, do you?" She grinned right back. Thea couldn't help herself. It surprised her how difficult it was to stay angry with him. Not to mention how at ease she felt when only hours ago she'd thought him capable of trying to kill her.

"How do you know my brother?" she asked, hoping to catch him off guard and finally get answers to the questions racing through her mind.

She watched as his face went from playful to serious in a flash. His brows furrowed as he thought. She knew in that second that whatever he told her would be the truth. He was only taking the time to say it as gently as he could. She admired him for that, but part of her just wanted for once to hear the unabridged version and not the watered-down, what-he-thought-the-princess-could-handle edition.

"I was his bodyguard."

And Leo had been shot. He didn't say it, but she could tell he was thinking it. The guilt flashed across his face as he spoke the words. Maybe not so much for his own feelings, but perhaps because of what he imagined she'd think of him.

"Do you think I'm going to blame you for his being shot?" Thea folded her hands in her lap to keep from reaching over and smoothing the worry from his face.

"Don't you?" His shoulders slumped slightly, so slightly anyone else might not have noticed. But she had spent the past fourteen years of her life studying people, determining who was telling her the truth and who was lying to protect her supposed tender feelings. In that moment she knew she couldn't be angry with him.

"Of course not." She couldn't blame him any more than those who had been trained to give up their lives for her and her family. Her heart broke for those who had already done so. Those men were so filled with duty and honor, they would never hesitate in doing what needed to be done. She was tired of the death, of the threats. She wanted it all to end.

She loved her brother more than anything. Without thought, her fingers found the medallion in her pocket and slowly began rubbing what was left of the raised surface of her family crest. He was all she had left. If he'd died, she would have lost a large piece of herself. Her life would have had an emptiness that would have taken a lot of time and prayer to ease.

"How did it happen?" Thea knew it would be uncomfortable for him to share and just as uncomfortable to hear. But she had to know. For now this man was her only connection to her brother. She reached across the space between their seats and lay her hand on his arm. She sensed the muscles in his forearm tense. "Please tell me."

Thea was relieved Ronin kept his eyes on the road. It was bad enough he could hear the emotion in her voice; she didn't want him to see the feelings she was sure were not hidden at all on her face. She closed her eyes and waited, praying that he would give her at least a little of what she needed so badly.

She didn't have to wait long.

"I don't know for sure how much you know

of your brother. But he has become a man with a huge heart. He tends to follow it into places he probably shouldn't."

Thea smiled. She pulled her hand back and relaxed into the passenger seat. His words brought back images and memories of the teenage boy Leo had been before their lives had changed. The few occasions she had seen him since had hardly been enough time to judge the man he had become.

"He has hidden himself away the last year or so working in a homeless shelter in Chicago," Ronin continued. "He's made quite a few friends there. He considers himself one of them."

"Because he understands what it's like to be without a place to call home," Thea remarked. It made perfect sense to her. Leo would experience a bond with those who didn't feel as if they belonged.

"Yes," Ronin agreed. "That's the way he explained it, as well."

"But how did he end up being shot?" Thea urged him to continue.

"One of his friends at the shelter went missing. Leo started investigating."

"On his own?" she asked.

"That surprises you?"

"No, not really." She sighed. "I probably would have done the same thing."

"I had just made contact with your brother. Leo had already been at it a few weeks. He was close to a breakthrough, I imagine."

"And that's what got him shot?"

"We think so."

"So it wasn't the same people who are after me?" It seemed bizarre that so much danger had come into their lives at the same time but for different reasons.

"As far as we can tell." Ronin paused for a few moments and gripped the steering wheel tightly as an eighteen-wheeler attempted to pass them on the slick road. "He has people with him looking into it to be sure."

"Could you have done anything to stop it?" she questioned.

"I did all that I could."

"Then you have your answer. It's not my place to judge what you could or couldn't have done."

"How can you be so forgiving?"

Thea didn't have to think long. The answer was easy. She'd learned holding on to bitterness and blame brought only pain. The only way to truly live a happy life was to forgive.

"How can I not?"

* * *

Forgiveness was not something he was accustomed to.

Especially not so quickly and easily. He had done all that he could to protect Leo, but he'd been just that much too slow. He had been busy watching for an attack from those in power in their country; he hadn't expected it from some random source. But still, he'd failed and he did blame himself for that.

He would not fail a second time.

He glanced over at the woman next to him. Thea truly was special. At first glance she might seem rather ordinary if you didn't know of her heritage. A tiny jagged scar high on her forehead was the only feature keeping her face from being perfect. If you took the time to look deeper than surface impressions, you could see true beauty.

Wavy locks of deep chestnut hair framed a lightly freckled face. He knew from his research that she hated the freckles. But they gave her character. She was beautiful, but it was her inner beauty that shone through more than anything.

She had her father's faith, as well. When she'd asked him if he believed in God, he hadn't been sure what to say. He believed. He knew there was a God, but his faith had wavered so much since the day they'd come for his father. His friends and his country had turned their backs not only on him, but on his brothers also. He couldn't help but think perhaps God had turned His back, too.

He glanced over at Thea and she smiled at him. She might still have her doubts and questions, but he could sense her trust. She was her father's daughter in every aspect. The king had been a wise man. King Donovan had ruled his people not with an iron fist, but with love. His kindness and faith had made the small country the prosperous land it was. When it was believed that the king and his son and daughters had been killed, his people had mourned the loss greatly.

It was perhaps that state of mourning that had allowed the king's second cousin, Marcus Wendell, to step in and take over the throne. During these past fourteen years, their country had been under King Marcus's rule, and the nation had very slowly been on a downward spiral. That spiral was attributed mostly to the fact that the king was weak-minded. For the past few years he'd taken to finding a bride. That endeavor had led him to his engagement with a woman of questionable character, Lucia Delmont.

At first Lucia had fooled them all. Mostly because during the first months of the engagement, she'd wisely kept in the background. But recently, he'd given her more and more power despite the fact they were not even wed yet. It was then that her true colors had begun to show to those who were wise enough to see her for what she was. It was almost to the point now that the bitter woman was ruling the country through the king. When word had leaked to the people that the prince and princess might be alive, an outcry to discover the truth had begun.

Unfortunately, the rumor also gave the real killer of their father motive to find them first and see that they never made it back to their country. The people might think the king's murderer was in prison. But it was not the truth—Ronin knew it in his heart. He also knew the real killer would see the need to finish the job that had been started all those years ago. Leo would be a target as part of the royal bloodline. But Thea held the truths that could see the assassin brought to justice. She had seen the killer, and whether she remembered who it was or not, she would be hunted with a vengeance. That hunt had already begun. For now there were only rumors that the prince and princess were alive. Someone out there would go to any means to squelch those rumors and see that the heirs remained dead to their people.

Only this time their deaths would be of a much more permanent nature.

"How much do you know of what is happening in our country?" he asked. He'd thought she'd be kept up-to-date on most of the current affairs, but he wasn't sure.

"Not much. I was barely ten when I was taken away. Those I had contact with seemed to think it was best I only knew that my father, sister and brother had perished." She paused as if needing an extra boost of fortitude to continue. "It was only when I overheard them planning on moving my brother that I learned he was still alive."

"That must have been difficult for you." His mother had died when he'd been young, as well. His father and brothers meant the world to him. He would do anything for them. The realization gave him a new respect for her and what she had overcome.

"It was." She sighed. "But I had my faith. I've always believed that good can come from the most difficult times. I had God with me through it all, and as Leo and I grew older, we also grew smarter. We found ways to work around the plans to keep us apart."

"By having your annual meeting?"

"Yes." Her voice broke. Ronin resisted the urge to reach out and lay his hand over hers. "It wasn't much, but it was better than never seeing my brother again."

"You will see him again." He hoped his words would give her the added courage to continue telling him what she knew. There was so much buried in her mind somewhere. She had been there when the king had been shot. No one knew for sure how much she'd witnessed, but anything at all would be better than the nothing he had now. He needed to know if she held any memory of his father from the night her family had died, if she remembered who had attacked her and left her for dead.

"I know." She sounded sure, more sure than he was at this moment. Where the courage came from he didn't know, but he respected her all the more for not giving up.

"What about you? Do you have family?"

"Yes. I have two brothers."

"Are they in Portase?"

Her question caught him off guard. He had hoped to get answers from her, not the other way around. Not that he minded sharing with her. He held a close bond with his brothers. They had come to the United States even before he had, when the country they had called home for all of their lives had shunned them.

"They are all here in the States, actually. My older brother, Jarrod, started up his own security company in Colorado. My other brother, Declan, and I have both been working for him."

Ronin debated telling her more. His father had gotten them both out alive and a plan had been set in motion before he was imprisoned. It was Jarrod's company that had provided the security for the prince and princess for the past several years. Before that, a few close friends of their father's had helped move Thea and Leo from place to place. It had become his family's mission to keep the royal heirs safe and hidden from those who were currently in power and were likely responsible for the king's death.

"Are you not from Portase, then?" Her voice sounded tired. She turned toward him and he noticed her stifled yawn. She was doing her best to stay awake, but she looked drained. After all that she'd been through today, she was probably exhausted both mentally and physically.

"Originally, yes." Any other truths he needed to share or questions he needed to ask could wait. "But that is a long story and you need to rest." It would be selfish to keep her awake when she so obviously needed sleep. "I'm going to drive as long as I can through the night. If you'd like to relax, there's a pillow and a blanket in the backseat."

"I might take you up on that," she said as she twisted in the seat, reaching behind her and feeling around for the items. Finding them, she turned and arranged the pillow against the window and her shoulder. She spread the heavy military blanket over her lap and snuggled into the seat as best she could. "Normally, I can't sleep in a moving car, but this snow is hypnotizing. Besides, I feel pretty safe with you at the wheel."

She would be safe. He'd see to that. Earlier he had not been paying as close attention to their surroundings as he should have been, and he'd nearly failed his self-imposed assignment before it even began. He honestly hadn't expected an attack so soon. He should have known better. But in those few minutes when she'd turned to face him, her eyes filled with trust, and he'd taken his mind off protecting her and thought about the many reasons she'd have for not trusting him when all of the truth came out.

Thea relaxed her head against the pillow and fidgeted some more, trying to find a comfortable position in near impossible circumstances. She would be asleep within minutes.

Ronin glanced in the rearview mirror to see if any vehicles were following. The men would need a new car, and they could have been in-jured and possibly arrested. The roads were nearly vacant with the ice storm picking up force in the area. Travel would be slow, but he and Thea had a good head start, and if they stuck to back roads, the odds were in their favor they would not be found.

"Is anyone back there?" she whispered.

"I thought you were asleep." He smiled and shook his head. He would have to be careful with her. She paid a lot more attention to things than he'd thought. "Nothing but ice and snow." He glanced back again, just to be sure. "Go to sleep. I'll wake you when we get there."

"Where's there?" she mumbled.

"We're headed to a safe house in Denver. Then, after your identity has been verified, it's on to the royal estate outside Denver."

"I've always wanted to see the mountains." She breathed the words on a sigh. Ronin wasn't sure if she was even awake.

When she didn't say anything else after a few minutes, Ronin realized she must have truly fallen asleep this time. It was going to be a long night. At these speeds and with these road conditions, they probably wouldn't arrive until late tomorrow. If his brothers were on task, they would be preparing a safe haven for the princess. But he couldn't be certain what they'd find when they arrived. There had been one leak already; there could be more. She'd need her rest for the possible receptions they could receive.

As he drove, Ronin thought of checking in with his older brother. Jarrod had worked hard behind the scenes to make sure everything was prepared for their arrival. He was just as dedicated to finding the truth as Ronin. It would be nice to know what preparations were being made, but he dismissed the idea. Cell service was limited and he wasn't supposed to make any sort of contact.

They were on their own.

He'd known that before he'd come for her. There would be no formal move against the current king until the prince and princess could be brought forth and validated as the true heirs of the throne. There were many out there who would go to any extremes to keep that from happening. The king was still the king, and if he had a hand in the murder of her father, he would have the support of their country. At least until the truth was revealed.

Ronin drove for several hours, running

different scenarios through his mind as they moved out of Missouri and into Kansas. It all passed by in a blur of white. None of the ways Thea's homecoming might play out were within acceptable limits. Until their country actually saw them and accepted them, she and Leo were still as good as dead. He had no doubt attempts could be made on their lives even once they'd reached the estate where they were to meet. Until the real killer was found and imprisoned, they would never be safe.

He'd just made the decision to switch to a different county road that would be less traveled when he noticed the headlights coming up behind him. The only vehicles he'd seen in the past few hours were two truckers moving even slower than himself and a car that was being pulled out of a ditch by a tow truck.

The headlights came up fast behind him. Too fast.

Within moments the interior of the car was flooded with bright light.

Ronin watched in disbelief as the car grew closer. Only a desperate fool would try what he knew was about to happen.

"Thea." He spoke calmly but loudly. He didn't dare take his hands off the steering wheel to nudge her. "Thea, wake up."

Thea awoke with a start at the first lurch of the car when bumper tapped against bumper.

"What's happened?" she questioned, bolting upright in her seat and glancing quickly behind them.

"Hold on tight." Ronin gripped the steering wheel, preparing for the worst that was sure to come. "They've found us."

FOUR

Thea rubbed her eyes in an attempt to remove the last remnants of sleep. The interior of the car was lit up bright as day, but it couldn't be morning already. A quick glance through her window showed nothing but darkness against a haze of snow. She glanced over at Ronin. His knuckles whitened as his grip on the steering wheel tightened.

For a brief moment she thought she was still asleep, caught in some bizarre nightmare.

Her body lurched forward, the seat belt catching tightly around her waist and upper body.

Bright headlights flooded the inside of the car, blinding her as she turned to look behind them. This was very real.

Metal crunched against metal and she lurched forward again, feeling the car slide from one side of the road to the other.

"Brace yourself!" Ronin shouted. The car

slammed into them again. His expert handling of the wheel kept them from going into a total spin. For now anyway.

Panic welled up in her chest. Her first instinct was prayer. She wasn't sure if her mumbled words were aloud or in her mind, but they were from her heart. God was with her. He would keep them safe. She knew it. But the fear still threatened to overtake her.

Thea glanced over her shoulder and saw the car coming up on them again. Another crunch as the other car made impact with their rear fender. Ronin fought with the steering wheel, struggling to keep the car on the road. His eyes darted between the mirrors and the road ahead. His body tensed with every motion. A frown covered his features as the car moved up beside them, bumping them.

Side by side they raced at unsafe speeds down the icy road. In the darkness, she could barely make out the shapes of the two men in the car. A flash of metal caught her eyes as one waved what looked like a gun.

Ronin turned the wheel sharply, effectively ramming his car against theirs. The car slid away from them and then came back with force, screeching against them as each car pushed back against the other.

"This is crazy!" she yelled over the scraping of the cars.

She wasn't sure if Ronin could hear her. She could barely hear herself.

Ronin sped up and for a few moments kept some distance between them.

"You're going too fast." Driving these speeds on the icy roads would only endanger them more.

"They are not going to give up." He glanced at her quickly, his eyes filled with concern.

The car came up beside them again, ramming hard into the driver's side.

"We're going to go off the road." He said it as fact, giving her some warning of what was about to happen. "Hold on."

Thea felt the slide as the car rammed them one last time. There would be no controlling it. She watched helplessly as they crossed the edge of the pavement, plowing through guardrails and heading down a steep embankment. Thea grabbed tight at the edge of her seat with one hand and the handgrip with the other as the car jostled from side to side. Her head knocked against the passenger-side window, sending jolts of pain through her body.

Twigs and barbed wire scratched against her window as they flew through a fence and farther down the incline. The car jerked and then tipped. She closed her eyes as the car rolled hard to one side. Her seat belt pulled tight against her, digging into her skin as she was tossed in every direction as the roll continued.

The air bag shot out against her chest at the same time the car landed with a deafening thud and splash at the bottom. Water seeped over her feet.

They were in water. Freezing water.

Thea sucked in a deep breath and choked on the dusty, chemical-filled air. Stabs of pain shot through her lungs as she did so.

"Are you okay?" Ronin asked. She nodded, but even that slight movement sent more pain shooting through her body. She was nowhere near okay, but she was alive. That in itself was no small feat considering the situation. God had His hand on them. Of that she was sure.

"We need to go," he said.

Movement seemed nearly impossible when every breath she sucked in brought more pain, but she knew they had little choice. If the men who had run them off the road hadn't suffered a worse fate, they would be looking for them. They had left little doubt about their determination. The thought spurred her movements and she reached around to unclasp her seat belt. But pressing the release button repeatedly brought no satisfaction.

"It's stuck." She tugged as hard as she could. "My seat belt is stuck."

Thea continued to struggle with the clasp. Panic welled up inside her along with visions of the water rising to cover her.

"It's okay." Ronin's large, warm hands closed over hers, tugging with her, but to no avail.

His hand moved away and for a slight moment the thought darted through her mind that he meant to leave her. But within seconds he was back. Thea barely registered the flash of steel as the blade of a knife. She felt a tug and heard the slice through the cloth constraint. The release of pressure was instantaneous. She was free.

"You can breathe now."

"I am breathing," Thea replied as she released the breath she'd not realized she'd been holding.

Ronin didn't argue as he reached over her, slashing through the now-deflated air bag to reach the glove compartment. It was too dark to make out the objective of his fumbling movements, but within seconds his attention was elsewhere.

"Grab anything you have to help stay warm." He reached behind her and tossed her bag into her lap. His voice strong and steady, he continued, "If you have gloves or a scarf, put them on."

She did as she was told, thankful that she'd thought to pack all the things he mentioned.

"Make sure you have your adrenaline auto-injector with you. We may not come back to the car." The fact that he knew her so well and thought to remind her surprised her; she was in such a state of shock she wouldn't have thought of it. His calmness soothed her.

She took a deep breath.

"Can you get your door open?" he asked.

Thea tested the handle and felt the pop of the latch as she pulled on it. "I think so." With a slight nudge of her shoulder, the door creaked open.

"Good. Mine is jammed."

Thea stepped out into water. Mixed with chunks of ice, the frozen slush seeped through her boots and soaked the bottom of her jeans. Thankfully, the water was only shin deep and after a few wobbly steps she was able to stand. She moved along the side of the car and could feel Ronin right behind her, his hands on her back and head, pushing her gently over into a hunched position behind the car.

"Stay low," he whispered, tossing the blanket over her shoulders as he glanced above her head.

Snow still fell in huge flakes. Thea looked around them to see if the other car and the men in it were nearby, but visibility was limited. The wind blew in forceful gusts, sending the snow dancing in clouds of frozen swirls. He held her close as he tugged the blanket tight across her back and shoulders, pulling her against him in his temporary warmth. For a moment they were alone in their own little world.

"Keep this around your neck and up over your face," he said. His gloved fingers brushed her cheek as he adjusted the knitted scarf.

Warmth filled her despite the freezing conditions. She allowed herself to feel safe and protected as she looked up into his eyes. Tiny bits of snow and ice caught in his lashes and along his brow as he glanced at her and then their surroundings.

"I think they went off on the other side of the road," Ronin said.

Thea shivered. She was soaked, bruised and freezing, but she knew he would stop at nothing to keep her safe. That was what he had been trained for. To protect her. To lay down his life for her if need be. Just like those who had protected her before had done. Part of her wanted to pull away and run into the arms of those who wanted her dead. Just to end it all.

"Don't let go of my hand." The warmth of his hand closed around hers as he took it.

She gripped tightly. She wouldn't let go. Despite the fear and pain, giving up now would make all that had happened before this moment be for nothing. Those who had already died deserved more than her quitting.

The wind gusted against them, making movement even more difficult. She was thankful for the wind and snow. The blizzard conditions could keep them hidden, if the freezing temperatures didn't kill them first.

Ronin tugged Thea along behind him, her small hand lost in his. He felt her shiver, and with each shake of her body he willed every ounce of heat from his body through his gloved fingertips to try to give her some warmth. She was strong, probably stronger than she knew, but if he could take the pain for her, he would. She didn't deserve this.

Thea stumbled and he slowed his pace. A full moon hung high in the sky, but it didn't provide them much light through the heavy clouds. A constant sheet of snow blew against them. Each step felt like a battle through a wall of freezing foam. The wind made travel more difficult, but it also blew across their tracks, making it nearly impossible for anyone to follow them. Yet every time he glanced behind them, he could see beams of light slicing through the white haze. The eerie glow only reminded him of how much danger they were in.

Ronin pushed forward, half dragging her behind him. She stumbled again, but this time the full weight of her body pulled against him. He turned to realize she'd slid on the edge of a small ravine; her body hung like deadweight as she fought for a foothold to help herself up.

A strong gust of wind blew as Ronin tugged against her arm and he lost his footing as well, sending them both tumbling the short distance to the bottom.

"Are you okay?" he asked, gathering her up in his arms.

"I'm sorry. I should have been more careful."

"It's not your fault." Ronin glanced around and spotted a tiny crevice against the ravine wall that was barely large enough for two people to squeeze into. "Can you make it over there?" he asked pointing toward the large, gnarled tree roots that hid the entrance.

At her nod they made their way. Ronin dusted off a spot of rocky ground and then sat with his back against the stone wall. He pulled her down beside him, wrapping the blanket around them both so that they were totally covered except for the small slit he left at his eyes. The heavy wool material would shield them from the snow and give them some warmth as it held in their combined body heat.

"We'll rest for a few moments."

She needed the time. He knew that, but just as certainly he knew if they stopped for very long, they'd be dead. The men who had run them off the road meant business. They were not here to take prisoners. Not the way they'd slammed into them.

It didn't make sense. His mind raced. He had taken extra care to stay on back roads. Even though they were less maintained and more hazardous with the worsening weather, avoiding as much traffic as possible made it less likely they'd be noticed.

He'd been even more careful since they'd been on foot. He'd stayed near the creek until it had veered back toward the road. For the past half hour or so, they'd ducked in between trees and overgrowth in a densely wooded area.

She wiggled closer to him and he tightened his arm around her and held her close. The blanket cocooned them both. He could feel the warmth slowly beginning to heat his limbs.

"What's that?" she asked.

"That" could mean any number of things,

but knowing she was snuggled up against his left side, he was pretty sure of what she'd noticed.

"That's my gun."

"You have a gun?" Her voice shook. Whether from the cold or fear, he wasn't sure. "You've had a gun all this time?"

"It was in the glove compartment." He'd left it there when he'd gone to meet her. Maybe he shouldn't have, but he hadn't wanted to take the risk that she'd see it and be even more afraid of him than she had been.

"Are you going to shoot them?"

Would he? In a heartbeat.

"Only if I have to," he replied.

He felt her relax against him again. Happy his answer seemed to have pacified her, his focus returned to the men who were hunting them. They'd steadily been gaining on them. Soon, they'd be within earshot.

It went against his every instinct to stay hidden. He could take them. He knew it. He would have the benefit of surprise. He had his gun. Although he was reluctant to use it in anything less than a life-and-death situation, he was reasonably sure it would come to that if they were found. However, they had probably been injured also. It served them right. He knew it was wrong to think it, but he only hoped they suffered more. Considering what they'd already put Thea through, he'd enjoy having a part in some of that suffering.

Her strength continued to amaze him. After what she'd experienced, he wouldn't be surprised if she took his gun from him and shot them herself. There was only so much a person could take. He'd seen it before—what a person could be like when they reached that limit. Her father and sister had been taken from her, and she'd spent her teenage years moving from one home to another, never having time to form friendships or fall in love.

She'd lived in fear, waiting and wondering if someone would come for her.

She had to be pretty close to that edge.

That realization gave him the clarity to stay right where he was. More important than seeing the people against her punished was the fact he had to get her home safe. Hiding was the only option for now. If he showed himself, she'd be right behind him. He couldn't put her in that danger. He had to protect her. He had to find out what she remembered of that night.

There was every chance he'd bring her more pain. When she discovered he'd come for her not only to protect, but also to guard and retrieve the knowledge she held in her mind, she might never trust him again. It was a chance he had to take.

He held her close. She trusted him now. That would have to be enough.

FIVE

Thea huddled against Ronin, fighting the feelings of despair that sought to overtake her. She was cold. Every part of her body hurt. She'd really had about all she could take tonight. So many times through the years she'd thought she'd come to the end of her rope, but God had always given her strength to keep moving forward. She feared more than the men who were trying to kill her. She feared fear itself. There was really only one option available to her other than letting the fear take over.

She prayed and relaxed back into Ronin's warmth.

She wiggled her fingers free from her glove just long enough to find the medallion buried in her pocket. Her father had given it to her. It was all she had left of him. Her fingers rubbed over the smooth metal, filling her mind with the memories she'd held dear for such a long time.

Seconds passed. The sounds of the wind

and Ronin's breathing against her ear were all she heard. He held her against his chest. The blanket covered her and gave her much-needed warmth but also left her in total darkness. It was easy to imagine she was invisible. If the men did come this way, they'd walk right on by without seeing them.

She huddled closer.

In the darkness she could only imagine. She imagined the men who were after them growing closer. Rustling sounds of branches creaking as the wind blew surrounded her. A large crack ripped through the night air as a branch, weighted with the heavy snow, broke. Suddenly sounds were all around her. But it was what she couldn't hear that scared her the most.

Thea tried to shake the fear away. She focused on her faith and the prayers she knew had been heard. She focused on Ronin's strong arms around her. He'd protect her. That only gave her more reason to fear. Visions of the man who had died for her just last week flashed in her mind. After her shift at the diner, she'd returned to the safe house to find his body on the ground. He'd used his last ounce of strength to order her to run.

She'd run. She'd run and left him to die.

She would not run again. If she had to, she'd

jump out and pummel the men herself with whatever she could find.

Despite her newfound determination, her body shook with a mixture of fear and cold. The temperature at least gave her something to focus on. Her toes had gone numb. She shuffled slightly, trying to get to a position where she could rub her feet, possibly bringing some circulation back.

"Be still," Ronin whispered, his breath warm against her ear.

Seconds later she heard voices. At first she thought she'd only imagined the sound. The wind howling through the trees had an uncanny voice-like quality.

The crunching sound of footsteps through the snow accompanied the voices. She ducked as low as she could inside the confines of Ronin's arms and froze in place. She barely dared breathe as the voices drew closer. Gone was all the fearlessness she'd felt only moments before.

"Do you still have it?" a low voice asked. The sound was so close it startled her and she flinched. Ronin motioned above them to the ledge she'd fallen from.

"No." The single word was followed by barely coherent swearing. "This storm isn't helping."

"It's not supposed to help you. You do know

what you're doing, don't you?" The first voice grew more and more impatient.

For a brief moment there was only rustling sounds of clothing to indicate they were still near. Then the second voice spoke again. "I've lost it. I think it was coming from over in that direction."

There were more crunching and rustling sounds. Thea held very still, hoping they weren't pointing toward them.

"Think?" the first man said with an indignant pitch. "We're not getting paid to think. We're getting paid to bring her back. Dead or alive."

"I know, I know," the other man replied in a younger, whiny tone. "But there's no way anyone can survive the night out here. If she's not dead already, she will be by morning."

"Agreed. We're supposed to bring back a body, though. Not just leave her lying around where someone might find her. There can be no proof that she was alive."

The younger man let out a few more choice words. "Maybe we can get a body somewhere else?"

Thea cringed. That they were capable of that sort of thought and action both shocked and terrified her.

"Don't be stupid." Her heart pounded in her

chest and for a moment she worried the sound would give her away. "We're going to do this right."

Snow crunched as they shuffled around on the ledge above them. They were so close she could hear their heavy breathing.

"What about him?"

"No one cares."

"But he's one of us."

"He *was* one of us," the older man shouted out loudly as the wind picked up in howling blasts again. "He chose his side."

"If she's dead out here, no one is finding the body anytime soon. I say we head back."

"You're probably right. Make sure you have the coordinates and we'll come back when the snow melts if we have to. This is ridiculous and I need a doctor. I think I broke my arm."

The voices were already sounding more distant, either from the wind or movement. Thea was glad she'd no longer have to listen to such wickedness.

Even after the sounds of them leaving had subsided, Thea sat perfectly still. She played each word she'd heard over and over again in her mind. With each passing moment the blanket over her head grew heavier as the snow accumulated on it. She focused on every breath, keeping it as slow and quiet as possible. She resisted the urge to throw the blanket off and run, forgetting her earlier vow to never run again. Fighting seemed so futile. Everyone wanted her dead. Would she even be safe when she returned home?

Ronin's arms tightened around her as if sensing her fear and uncertainty.

For so many years she'd lived with the knowledge that someone wanted her dead. Even in that knowledge she'd somehow felt distanced, as if it wasn't really happening to her, as if it was only a memory or a possibility. Since the death of her father and younger sister, she'd lived in a bubble of protection. She and her brother had been kept safe until a time when they would be old enough to handle the responsibility of the throne. To learn now that those who meant to harm her might have known where she was all along only opened up more questions.

There had to be a reason why the danger had become real these past few days. Ronin knew the answers. She was sure of it. The men had said Ronin had been one of them. Her mind raced with the possible meaning of their words and with the fear the men might return. As proud as she was that she had learned to protect herself, she was no match for anyone now. She had no silly brick-filled bag with her. She had only Ronin. The men's hateful words reminded her she didn't even know who he was.

Thea pushed back the hopelessness that threatened to fill her. Through all the years, she'd never allowed herself to feel sorry for herself and she wasn't about to start now. God hadn't brought her this far to leave her to freeze in the middle of nowhere. Some people trusted their gut. Thea trusted her heart. Despite the words she'd overheard, she knew in her heart Ronin was a good man. He was a little rough around the edges, but a good man nonetheless.

Thea whispered a prayer, more to herself than aloud, but she knew without a doubt it had been heard as a sense of peace flooded her. Ronin had been sent to her for a reason. She would get through this.

Thea felt around for something she could use to protect herself with, should the need arise. Her gloved fingers moved over the snow-covered ground slowly and rubbed up against a small branch. Her fingers wrapped around it tightly and she listened to the sounds around her. She strained her ears, searching for any indication of the men's return. There was only the howling of the wind and her and Ronin's breathing. It filled her ears. In and out. In and out.

"They've gone. You're safe now," Ronin said softly, but still his voice startled her.

She rose slowly, allowing him to help her to her feet as they heaved the snow off the blanket that had been covering them.

His words rung in her ears, over and over. *You're safe now.* The words took her back to that night when she'd been rescued from the closet. Strong arms had held her tight then, too, and carried her through her burning home to safety. Over and over he'd said those same words to her and she'd known he was telling her the truth. But it was more than the words; it was the voice. The familiarity of it clawed through her mind.

She brushed the remaining snow from her shoulders. She'd never learned who that man had been, but she imagined he would have been a lot like the man in front of her.

"Were you planning on hitting me again?" he asked, his eyes darting to the stick she held by her side. He was only inches away from her. She fought the urge to throw her arms around him and hold him close. She already missed the warmth and the feeling of protection his arms had given her. She wanted him to keep telling her everything was going to be all right. When he did, it somehow made her want to believe even more. But the men's words still blared in her mind.

"Should I?" she questioned.

Thea regretted the words the moment she spoke them. The warmth and compassion faded from his face.

"Do you really still think I want to hurt you?" His eyes burned with an emotion she couldn't name. All she knew was it was very deep and something he struggled to control.

"No." If he meant to hurt her, if he was really one of them, he'd had plenty of time before now to do so. She dropped the stick as she spoke. "I trust you."

She did trust him, but so many unanswered questions still raced through her mind. Thea gave voice to the one that screamed loudest.

"What did they mean when they said you were one of them?" Ronin stiffened. He had to know she'd ask, but he seemed caught off guard by her pointed question. He looked away and she stepped closer to him.

"What did they mean?" she asked again. A shiver shuddered through her body as the wind picked up.

"It's very complicated and you are freezing." Ronin shook the remaining snow from the blanket and once again draped it over her shoulders. "We need to get moving again and find shelter."

"What we need is for you to uncomplicate it." Thea stiffened to match his posture. He knew a lot more about what was going on than he'd shared. That was about to change. "I'm not moving until you tell me."

"I could carry you." His head tilted to one side in challenge.

She mulled the idea over. She did like the way his arms felt around her, but it was past time for some straight answers. "Then carry me." She called his bluff.

He faced her, his hands on his hips.

Thea stood her ground. He might think to intimidate her with his bold stance, but she was determined. The snowstorm could blow giant drifts over her before she'd leave this spot without answers.

He stared deep into her eyes. She met his gaze confidently, not giving him an ounce of the timidity he looked for. He sighed and threw his hands up in the air.

"Short version," he relented. "Then we go. I have no desire to watch you freeze to death."

She nodded and waited.

"My family was Royal Guard."

"Royal Guard? Were those men Royal

Guard?" she questioned. They had said he'd been one of them. "Are my own people trying to kill me? Answer me. Is my own Royal Guard after me to kill me?"

His brows drew together in an agonized expression. She knew the answer before he even said it.

"Yes. For now they are not *your* Royal Guard. They are under the orders of the king. If he wants you dead, they will kill you."

"You think the king is behind the murder of my father and the attempts on my life?"

The muscles at his jaw tensed and relaxed. "It's a possibility."

He reached out his hand. Thea hesitated before taking it. She did trust him, but she still had questions.

"You had to choose between the Royal Guard and me, didn't you?"

She didn't really need to ask. She knew it to be true. It stung that he'd had to make that choice. But she was glad he'd chosen to help her rather than kill her.

"I made my choice years ago, Thea."

There was more that he wasn't telling her, she was sure. But she'd already learned more than her brain could process for now. "I guess we'd better get moving, then, before I truly do freeze to death."

* * *

Ronin stamped down the conflicting emotions Thea's questions had brought to the surface. He should explain more to her. He should tell her his father was one of the men who knew she was alive. That he was the one who had rescued her when she was a child and he'd been a huge part of keeping her safely hidden away.

Even when they'd imprisoned him and threatened to have him put to death for the murder of the king, he'd kept the secret.

She sensed it. He could tell every time she looked at him that she was remembering. He'd always been so much like his father. Even after all these years, she had to be noticing the similarities. It was a good thing. If being a reminder of the man who had saved her triggered more memories of that night, they could be that much closer to bringing the real murderer to justice.

He should explain all those things. But now was not the time or place. She had put him on the spot and he hadn't liked that at all. Not to mention she could freeze to death if he didn't find shelter for them soon.

He pulled Thea along behind him again as they made their way slowly out of the ravine. The snow still fell heavily, making each step even more difficult than the last. When they reached the top of the hill, he could see lights in the distance. The horizon glowed through the snow as the sunrise signaled the start of another day. He wasn't sure what they were headed for, but they would be out of this weather.

He pressed on, feeling a surge of victory.

Thea would be warm and safe and he'd have a chance to tell her the rest of the story she was so desperate to hear. She deserved to know it all. He was certain that somewhere in her mind were the answers he needed to find those responsible for not only killing her father, but also trying to silence his. Only when the truth came out would she finally be out of danger. Then he could return her home.

"I think there's a farmhouse up ahead." He spoke loudly over the wind, hoping to encourage her to keep moving. He quickened the pace and within moments they were at the door of the two-story home.

Ronin banged loudly against the door. The curtain at the window fluttered and lights came on inside. A few minutes later the door creaked open slowly. He was never so happy to see other human beings.

"Hello—" He started to introduce himself

but was interrupted as the lady at the door noticed their condition.

"Oh, my!" she exclaimed. "You two are a sight. You must be frozen all the way through."

Without taking time to learn their names or why they were out in the cold, she ushered them in and motioned for them to sit in the chairs around the kitchen table.

"Our car went off the road—" Ronin started, but was once again not allowed to finish.

"The nearest road is a good mile from here," the woman interrupted again. "That's quite the walk, especially in the middle of the night through a blizzard. First thing we need to do is get you out of those wet clothes." She clucked around them like a mother hen, urging them to sit in chairs around the table and remove their shoes. "Just pile those shoes and socks up in the corner there." She pointed toward a doorway that looked as if it led to a washroom. "Earl!"

"No need to holler, woman." A large man entered the kitchen, his arms full of blankets and towels. "One step ahead of you."

"We make a good team, don't we?"

The man laid the stack on the table and leaned over to give the woman a kiss on the cheek. The man might be older, but he was the same height as Ronin with a slightly heavier build. Ronin was well aware that although the man doted on his wife and had paid them very little obvious attention, he'd been measured up.

Ronin respected him for that. Given the circumstances, he'd do the same. He probably wouldn't have let two strangers into his home to begin with.

"We only have one bathroom and bathtub, so you'll have to take turns at warm baths. But we have a tub around here somewhere that you can soak those feet in."

The man—Earl, she'd called him—was already leaving the room again.

Thea still shook from the cold. Ronin was worried for her feet. They had been out in the freezing temperatures for hours. She could have frostbite. But you couldn't tell by looking at her. She smiled at the woman and thanked her, not once complaining or letting on about the pain she must be in.

"We were in an accident." Ronin supplied the information, for the first time not being interrupted. "Our car landed in a creek."

"Must have been Rock Creek." The woman shook her head and made more clucking sounds as she helped Thea with her boots and socks.

Ronin leaned over as he pulled his own off

to see if her toes showed any signs of being blistered.

"God must have been with you two," the woman replied. "If you've been out in that cold for very long. He had His hand on you to keep you safe."

"He did." Thea spoke with a calmness that surprised him. She smiled up at him. "Of course, Ronin helped some, as well."

A smile filled his body. Contagious warmth flowed from her.

The elderly man returned to the room with a large metal tub and began filling it with warm water from the sink.

"I'll show you to the bath and find some warm, dry clothing for you to put on while your own clothes are drying out." The woman wrapped her arms around Thea and guided her out of the room.

At the doorway, Thea stopped and glanced back at him. Her eyes filled with softness.

Thank you, she mouthed. Then she was gone.

"That lady of yours is one strong woman." The man placed the partially filled tub down at Ronin's feet, then returned to the sink to begin filling pitchers of warm water to add to it. "Reminds me of my own Elizabeth. She has that same stubborn streak in her."

"She's not my lady," Ronin corrected. He didn't want to repay the man's kindness with lies. There had been too many lies already. Not that he had actually lied to Thea, but he'd kept the truth from her. And she had thanked him. Ronin sunk his feet into the warm water. His feet tingled, then sharp jabs of pain shot through his toes and up his legs. He jerked and grimaced.

"That's a good sign. Means the circulation is returning and your toes aren't completely dead."

He held his feet under. He deserved the pain.

"I'm going to see if Lizzie needs some help rounding you young'uns up some clothes." Earl looked down at him and then strode away after his wife.

He was right about Thea. She was a strong woman. She was strong and many more things that he wasn't sure there were even names for. A man could spend a lifetime trying to figure her out. He shook the thoughts from his mind. She was also a princess. It had been so easy for him to forget her heritage and who she really was in the time he'd been with her. For so long he'd thought of her only as a means to an end. The truths in her mind could free his father.

She was his duty, a job. Nothing more, nothing less.

The memory of the look in her eyes before she'd left the room flooded him. She trusted him. Despite the few truths he had shared and the questions that remained, she trusted. She knew his family had worked for the Royal Guard. She still trusted him. For now that was a good thing. He'd achieved part of what he'd set out to do.

He'd gained her trust. In the days to come he could very well crush it.

SIX

Thea would never again take a simple thing like a warm bath for granted.

She wrapped her hair in a fluffy pink towel and stared at the purple bruise along her chin. After a quick examination for other injuries, she dressed quickly in the oversize sweatshirt and sweatpants Lizzie had left for her. Her arms and legs were covered in bruises. Her ribs and right shoulder were bruised, probably from the seat belt or air bag. But nothing was broken.

Things could have been much worse. She'd thanked God several times since they'd entered the small farmhouse. She was alive. Ronin was alive.

They were safe.

For now. Thea pushed the errant thought to the back of her mind.

Mr. and Mrs. Hollis—or Earl and Lizzie, as they'd insisted on being called—had welcomed them in without hesitation. Lizzie had drawn a warm bath and set out clean clothes and towels, tending to her like family the whole time. She liked it. It had been a very long time since she'd felt that sort of caring. Her own mother had been that way. The attention reminded her of her mother's gentleness. It was something she'd nearly forgotten. For so long it had been only her father, Leo and their younger sister, Adriana.

After her mother had died, her father had dated a few women, but he'd never really brought them into their lives. Mostly there had been servants. Some of them had genuinely cared for her. But that had been different. It always felt more as if they were doing it out of obligation than true emotion. She was their job.

Thea tugged on the thick pair of socks. Warmth had finally returned to her toes, and thankfully, they looked pink and healthy. She wiggled them again just to be sure. She never wanted to be that cold again.

She jumped at a light rap at the door and then laughed at herself. If the men who were chasing them had returned, she doubted they'd knock.

"Are you okay?" Ronin's voice was filled with genuine worry.

"Yes, I'm fine." She could hear Ronin pacing

in the hallway. She smiled. She should have known he wouldn't be far from her side. "Are you?" she questioned.

He stopped pacing long enough to answer, "Yes."

"Are we safe here?" Thea moved toward the door, listening for any sound he might make. If he told her anything other than the truth, she would know. In the short time she'd known him, he'd gotten quite easy to read, even through a door.

"For now," he replied with a heavy sigh. "But we can't stay long."

Thea agreed with him. Eventually, the men would come after them. They wanted a body. Dead or alive, they'd said. She had no doubt they would keep searching until they were stopped or they'd succeeded.

Ronin would protect her for as long as he could. But why?

"If you are not the Royal Guard, then why are you here?" The question had been in the back of her mind all morning. He'd already admitted he was not with the Guard. But he'd said he was her brother's bodyguard.

Thea strained her ears. Windows rattled as gusts of wind from the storm still raging outside blew against them. She could hear him moving around outside the door. Was he thinking up lies to tell her? She dismissed it. He hadn't lied to her yet. He'd kept things from her, yes, but she didn't want to think he'd actually lie outright.

"I was a bodyguard for your brother for a short time, but not as a member of the Royal Guard," he said on a frustrated sigh.

Her mind raced. "I'm not sure if that really answers my question."

Thea waited, unsure if she would have to repeat herself or if he would finally get around to answering.

"The people who have been protecting you and your brother for the past several years haven't exactly been working for the king."

"Because the king could be the one who wants me dead." She sighed. He'd said as much earlier, but it still seemed so impossible. The man was family. Not closely related, but still family. That he could be the one behind her father's murder and the attempts on her life was unthinkable.

"Yes." Through the closed door she sensed the frustration in his voice. "The Guard sides with the king. Not that there aren't a few of them who doubt the legitimacy of his claim to the throne, but he is the king. There are those who work in secret, keeping you safe and waiting for the right time to bring you both home."

"Your brother's company?" she asked.

"Yes, and a few others who remained loyal to your father."

"But if the king is the one who is behind all of this, how can we ever go against him?" Thea questioned. She had always held tight to hope, but in this instant everything seemed hopeless. Thea tiptoed slowly toward the door.

Her own people meant to kill her. Those who had once vowed fidelity to her father were now the ones trying to end her life. Yet Ronin had protected her. "Then who sent you?"

"This is not a conversation to have through a door."

"It actually seems to be working just fine," she replied. It was probably one of their longest conversations. If not, at least the one that actually answered some of her questions. "Who sent you?"

"I sent myself, Thea."

Thea mulled his reply over in her mind.

Leaning against the door, she asked, "Why?"

"To bring you home safe." His answer was quick. Almost too quick. It sounded rehearsed. There had to be more to it than that.

"You said only a handful of people knew about my brother and I still being alive. Who else knows?"

She heard his sharp inhale. Then he began the pacing again.

"My father told me." She could hear him pacing in long strides. "My father was the head of the Royal Guard at the time of your father's murder. He told only a few of his most trusted men. Some of the people who kept you hidden didn't even know who you were. It was better that way."

"My bodyguards haven't been Royal Guard, then?" She thought of the men who had protected her, always following her, always watching. She had trusted them.

"No. They were private contractors."

She had thought they had protected her out of loyalty to her father and to her. To find out that they'd only done it for money somehow cheapened it.

Thea wasn't sure what to say. Learning the past fourteen years she'd lived not in the protection of her countrymen, those who cared for her and felt a devotion to her father, but those who had just been paid to do so left her speechless. It had been a lie of her own creation, but that didn't make it any easier to accept.

Thea placed her ear against the door. Partially to listen for him, but also because she needed the support it offered. The events of the past few hours hit her like a sledgehammer to the stomach. Her legs went limp. She slid down the door, leaning against it as she collapsed into a sitting position on the floor. She wrapped her arms around her body and willed herself to let go of all the pain that had been building. She hated crying, but it always made her feel better.

No matter how badly she wanted a good cry, though, no tears would come. She'd cried herself out years ago. Tonight had been a test of her faith. She'd always believed prayer was stronger than whatever could come against her. But tonight she'd felt real fear. She wasn't supposed to have fear. Fear was for people who didn't have faith to believe all things were possible. Yet she'd survived something that many people could have only imagined. In one night someone had tried to kill her not once but twice. That had to count for something.

Thea sat there in a heap of physical and mental exhaustion. She wasn't sure how much time had passed when she heard rustling outside the door.

"I'm going downstairs," Ronin muttered from the other side of the door.

He hadn't left yet. She wondered briefly if he were listening at the door as she had done, if he waited for her to make a sound. Part of her wanted to believe he was there because he cared for her. But now that the truth was coming to light, she could only believe he was there for the same reasons all the other men had protected her. She was nothing more to him than a job.

"I'll be down shortly," she replied to break the silence. She needed time alone before facing him.

There was mumbling from the other side of the door. She strained to listen but couldn't make out anything that he was saying. She probably didn't want to know.

She'd been a fool to think he considered her more than a paycheck when he'd held her and comforted her earlier. That he might actually really care what happened to her as a woman. She wouldn't let foolish thoughts like that blur her judgment again. If that was the way he wanted to be, she could play the part well. She could be the little princess who needed rescuing.

At least long enough to rescue herself.

She was through with people viewing her only as a parcel to be protected or delivered. She was a capable woman who could get herself to Denver. It couldn't be hard to find the royal estate. Once her people saw her, they would accept her and she could take her rightful place as an heir to the throne.

Thea pulled the towel from her head and ran her fingers through her damp hair.

The men in the woods had said they'd be back when the storm passed. She didn't doubt that for a second. If they came here, Earl and Lizzie would be in danger. Now there were more lives at risk than just her own and Ronin's. She couldn't let that continue.

They were safe for now, but as soon as possible she needed to get out of here and get herself to Denver, where she could put an end to this once and for all. If the king really was behind her father's death and the attempts on her life, there was only one way she could see to reveal it.

He would have to be caught in the act.

No one would believe it otherwise. Not without proof.

Those who had killed her father and tried to destroy her family would receive the punishment they'd for so long deserved. She would see to that.

On her own.

Ronin might think she needed him, but he was going to learn soon that she was more than capable of taking care of herself.

Ronin headed to the stairway. On the way downstairs, he checked every window, every door. Thea's voice stuck with him. She sounded scared and alone. She hadn't liked the answers to her questions, but she needed to prepare herself for what was to come. She'd be wise to continue to question. The men who worked for the Royal Guard now were not her friends. Despite the position of high honor, they could not all be trusted.

Being a member of the elite group had always been his dream. He might not be recognized as Royal Guard now, but in his heart it would always be his title. Just like his father before him and each of his two older brothers. They had all been raised to someday serve the king and his family. He had just turned seventeen and begun his first months of training in the junior guard when word had arrived that the king and his family had been killed. He remembered that night. He and his brothers had been reeling over their deaths, and then Thea had arrived. Her first stop on her journey to a new life had been his home. He doubted she remembered it.

She'd been in a state of shock, but she'd tried to hide it. Even then she'd been brave.

After a careful survey, he made his way down the staircase. The wooden steps creaked with each footstep. It wouldn't be easy at all for anyone to sneak up on them. Not that he planned on letting his guard down.

He took the steps slowly, learning the sound of each one. The room below was open to the bottom half of the stairs. His eyes swept over it, taking in every detail as he moved down into the spacious living area. Throw blankets and pillows covered a plush sofa, two smaller love seats and a recliner.

An eight-point deer head was mounted over the mantel of a large stone fireplace. A fire crackled in the hearth. Its warmth flooded the room. An empty rifle rack hung to the left of the deer. Various photos of younger men in uniform dotted the mantel and walls along with family pictures.

Earl stood by the fire, jabbing logs with a poker. A rifle with a long-range scope sat propped up against the wall next to him.

"Everything locked up tight?" the older man asked.

Ronin studied him. Earl didn't turn away from the fire, but Ronin didn't need to look into his eyes to read him. His back was straight, his shoulders tensed. Ronin knew age was not a determiner of ability. Despite the man's apparent lack of attention, he was very much aware of what was going on around him. He'd heard him checking the house and probably knew what he was up to.

"Is there anything you'd like to tell me, son?"

"I have a gun with me. It's loaded." Lying was not even an option. He'd come into this man's home. He had every right to know; Ronin owed that much to him for the kindness they'd already shown.

"That's quite the coincidence. So do I." The older man motioned toward the rifle.

"I noticed."

"Thought you might."

"I have no intention of using it. Or of giving it up," Ronin added.

"I might think less of you if you did." The older man took another jab at the fire, then turned to look at him. "Does this have anything to do with the accident or the lady upstairs?"

"It has everything to do with the accident. There are men after her who will stop at nothing to kill her."

"I thought it might be something like that. You both had that hunted look in your eyes when you first showed up."

"We don't mean you any harm, and we're very grateful to you and your wife for taking us in." Ronin hoped Earl would hear the sincerity in his voice and not throw them out into the cold. Leaving now would not be in Thea's best interest, but he felt he had to give the man the option. "But if you'd like us to leave, we will."

"Nonsense," the man retorted. "I'm a good judge of character. I wouldn't have let you through the door if I hadn't already decided what I needed to know."

"Military?" Ronin asked. The man had obviously served his country in some way and had been well trained. Some things couldn't be taught, though. Some things a man was just born with.

"Yes. Twelve years. I was a sniper most of that time with the Army Rangers. I'd have been there longer if I hadn't been shot and messed up my leg. My family needed me here at home anyway."

"A sniper? That's impressive."

"Just don't let it get you thinking I can't shoot close-up if I need to." Earl smiled.

"I will keep that in mind." Ronin relaxed. He was a pretty good judge of character, as well. This was a man he'd be happy to have on his side. If it came to choosing sides.

"Any chance I'm going to need to be doing some shooting?"

"Not tonight. The men who were after us

turned back a few hours before we headed this direction. They were injured."

"Did you have anything to do with that?"

"Not this time." Given the chance in the future, he might. He'd remember their voices. If they knew what was good for them, they'd stay far away. "Is there anything I can do to help?" He felt the need to pitch in and do his part.

"Was thinking of bringing some more wood in," the man replied. "If you're up for it, I wouldn't say no to some help with that."

"I don't mind at all." He was hoping for a chance to check the perimeter of the home now that he felt certain the inside was secure. It would be wise to have a good lay of the land. They had a long day ahead of them if they were going to stay here for the night. From the sounds of the storm still raging outside, they weren't going to be going anywhere anytime soon. He doubted anyone would come looking for them until after the storm blew over. Even then, it might take a few days to dig out.

"There should be a nice stack just outside the back door." The man motioned over his shoulder toward the back of the house. "If not, out by the barn I have a bunch stacked up. It wouldn't hurt to bring some of that up so we won't have so far to go if need be. Gotta keep this fire going. There's a good chance the power will go out if this storm keeps up."

Both men turned as Lizzie entered the room, her hands full of gauze and ointments. "I was just on my way to see if your little lady needed any bandages. Is she still upstairs?"

"Last I checked," Ronin replied. He didn't feel the need to yet again comment on how she wasn't his lady. The couple seemed determined to have it otherwise.

"Actually, here I am. Thank you so much for the bath and dry clothing."

He glanced up at the sound of her voice. The sight of her shocked him but only momentarily. She'd worn the oversize coat, a hat and a scarf across her face most of the night. The only time he'd seen her in regular clothing had been at the restaurant, and that had been from across a table. Not that what she had on now could really be called regular.

Wearing a royal-blue sweatshirt with bright red University of Kansas lettering across the front, she descended the stairs. Several sizes too big, the shirt hung nearly to her knees. The sleeves were rolled up to her elbows, but even then they drooped loose and baggy around her arms. The bright colors of the fabric brought out the pink stain of natural blush to her cheeks. She didn't have on a speck of makeup, but she didn't need it. She glowed.

Her natural beauty took his breath away. Even dressed down in baggy cotton sweats, she descended the stairs like the regal princess she was. Dark hair lay damp against her shoulders. A few drying wisps blew with her movement. Her fingers lightly brushed the painted banister as she took each step slowly. She had a little limp to her step that she covered well, but he knew she must be hurting.

"I'm fine, just a few bumps and bruises. The bath worked wonders on them. I don't know how I can ever thank you enough, Lizzie," she said.

As she spoke she held her chin high. Each step was taken with care and perfect posture. He wanted to take the few steps that separated them and help her. The urge to feel her small hand in his again, to offer her strength and support, was nearly overwhelming. But he held himself perfectly still. It wasn't until she reached the last step that he realized he'd been holding his breath.

He shook himself and moved toward the door.

"I'll get that wood now," he said as he stepped outside and closed the door behind him. Her laughter floated to him as he stood outside. A cold blast of air hit him, but the sound of her voice warmed him. Something inside sparked to life. It was the fact that she held the answers he needed to save his father, he told himself as he trudged through snowdrifts toward the woodpile. Now was not the time to think it could be anything else.

Head down, he gathered as much wood as he could carry. Thinking there could be anything else between them was ridiculous. She was a princess. She was royalty. She'd have no place in her life for a simple man.

SEVEN

Thea sunk into the soft couch in front of the fire. For the first time in weeks, she relaxed.

"Here you go, sweetie." Thea smiled as the lady handed her a cup of hot tea. "We need to get your insides just as warmed up as your outsides now."

Thea took a sip of the honey-sweetened liquid. "This is delicious. Thank you."

"You're more than welcome. I'm just glad you two were able to find your way here through that storm." Lizzie patted her leg as she sat beside her. "They're saying this is the worst storm we've had in decades. It's so late in the season, too. Just goes to show how unpredictable the weather here in Kansas can be. There's just no telling what might have happened to you if you'd wandered around out there for much longer."

"I think prayer had a lot to do with it." Thea spoke the words she knew to be true. She'd who he'd been. She just hadn't put two and together. There was no ignoring it now.

A floorboard creaked. Her gaze shot toward e sound, and there he stood. His eyes were rk with memories of his own. She saw a ash of emotion she couldn't quite put her finger on. She wasn't sure how long he'd been tanding there or how much he'd heard, but y the look on his face, she figured he'd heard enough.

Ronin. His voice had triggered the memories. His voice had been so familiar. *He* had been so familiar and now she knew why. It could be just some sort of odd coincidence, but something in the way he looked at her—as if she'd just stumbled upon something priceless—told her all that words could not.

The elderly woman followed her gaze as Ronin and Earl stepped into the room and deosited the logs in their arms by the fire.

"Thea was just telling me quite the story."

"Sorry to have missed that," Earl said as he abbed a few logs and tossed them on the fire. Hopefully, we'll have time for a recap later?"

"Oh, she barely got started." Lizzie chuck-. "I'm sure there is a lot more left to tell."

"Quite a lot more," Thea said softly, never ing her eyes off Ronin. So many questions

prayed nearly the whole time, and even though she'd been afraid, she'd known they would be okay.

"Prayer is a mighty weapon, stronger than any man, that's for sure," the woman stated. "Not that that man of yours doesn't seem like the capable sort."

Thea had no control over the blush that made its way to her cheeks. "He's not my man exactly."

"I shouldn't tease you." Lizzie smiled. "God has been watching over you two. I sensed it the moment I opened the door to you. And that man, whether he's yours or not, he reminds me a lot of my Earl when he was that age. You'll have to stay on your toes with that one." The woman chuckled, her eyes darting around the walls to the many pictures of her and her family at various stages of her life. "But it's well worth it all."

Thea's gaze followed Lizzie's around the room. Children of various ages smiled back from framed photos on the walls and shelves around the room.

"Are these all your children?" Thea asked.

"Children and grandchildren. They are the jewels of my life."

Thea took another sip of her tea. The warmth of it slid through her body. She longed for a family. The memories of her childhood and helping with her baby sister after her mother had died were her fondest memories. She hadn't had a chance to be around children since her father's death. But she had to hope she would know how to be a good mother. Someday.

"Being a mother is an amazing gift," Thea added.

"I wouldn't trade a second of it for any-thing." The woman pulled one of the throw blankets over her lap and relaxed against the plush back of the sofa. "Enough about me. Tell me something about you."

"I wouldn't know where to even begin."

"I'll let you choose, but I've always found the beginning to be the best part. And we do have all day. If the power goes out we might end up having a little campout here in front of the fire tonight."

Thea smiled. "That sounds fun." And it did. It sounded like the perfect sort of memory she could take away from this. Instead of all of the pain and fear she'd felt, this would be a keep-sake she could cherish.

"The beginning it is, then." Thea took a deep breath to steady her nerves and stared into the fire. Flames flickered and popped. Through the years she'd tried not to think of the night

her father had been killed. But th   an
came to her in dreams. Her skin wa   tw
the glow of the fire and she relaxed,
mind go back to that night and the   th
she did have.   da

Leaning into the sofa cushions, s   fl
her story. She shared what she remen   g
the sounds and voices. Most of it wa   s
in her mind. After all these years she   h
really certain of what was memory or   e
She remembered the sound of the gu
clearly. The fear that had grabbed her,
she'd sat frozen in the closet for what se
like forever, the smell of the smoke and t
heat from the fire raging outside her s
sanctuary. She'd nearly given up hope
then he'd come. The man who had gathe
up in his arms and told her it would b
She had felt safe. She remembered ve
of him other than his voice.

The voice she remembered had   p
sounding a lot more real the past fe
It sounded a lot like…It sounded
Ronin's.

Thea's eyes flew open at the r
She'd been stupid to not have notice
had been at the back of her mind a   le
but she'd dismissed it. He'd give
through the night. He'd told her   tak

rushed through her mind. So many questions she couldn't ask right now.

But she would.

"She didn't even get to how they met. I'm sure that will be the best part," Lizzie stated.

The lights flickered, dimmed and slowly glowed back to life.

"It's only a matter of time now," Earl stated. "Might as well start shutting things down. We're going to lose power soon. I'll see to the animals before we lose all the light we have."

"I can help," Ronin offered.

"Thank you, but you two need to get settled in, and it'll probably be quicker if I just do what needs to get done."

"And I'll gather up all the extra pillows and blankets we have." Lizzie eased herself up off the sofa and tossed the blanket over its back. "It looks like we're going to have that campout a little earlier than we thought."

"If you can stay awake, maybe we could roast some marshmallows in the fire and really make a night of it." The man gave the fire one last good poke and then placed the poker back in the rack.

"Such a grand idea!" the woman exclaimed, planting a kiss on her husband's cheek. "I knew there was a reason I married you."

"Now, Lizzie, we both know that's not the

only reason you married me." He winked, causing the woman to giggle and blush.

"You best be getting us some more wood and cool yourself off," she scolded, but the smile on her face made it apparent she was only teasing. They were obviously still very much in love.

Only after they were both gone did Thea dare speak the words that had been running through her mind.

"It was your father, wasn't it?"

"Yes," he answered. He'd known the truth would come out eventually. He was relieved she'd figured it out on her own. It meant she did have some memories of that night and there was hope that she could clear his father's name.

"Why didn't you say so when you were telling me about your father?" she questioned. She scooted to the edge of the sofa, her eyes expectant as she waited for his answer.

"I felt it was important for you to piece it together on your own." It was the truth. If she didn't remember on her own, then how would he ever know what her real memories were?

"Important?" She stood and slowly stepped toward the fire. Her gaze locked on it as if she was searching it for answers…or trying to gain more memories.

Ronin stood silent a few feet away. Flames danced and flickered. A log popped, sending sparks shooting. "I wanted to see if you would remember. Do you?"

Thea shook her head. "It was just the voice, his voice. I was watching the fire and thinking of that night and I heard it plain as day." She turned and looked at him. "Then I realized I'd been hearing that voice all night. That it was you. But that was crazy—it couldn't have been you."

Ronin sensed the moment she verged on panic. He'd pushed her too much. He should have told her the whole story from the very beginning and not risked the damage the memories returning could do.

Ronin stepped toward her. Wrapping his arms around her, he pulled her close. "It will be okay." He repeated it over and over.

"Don't say that. Don't ever say that again," she yelled, pushing against him. "That's what he said, you know. That it would all be okay. And look at us. Does this look okay?" she questioned, motioning around her. He knew she meant the circumstances and what tonight had put them through, but he was blind to everything but her.

Thea pushed away. Drawn to the fire, she reached her hands out, warming them near the flames. For a moment he worried she'd reach right into the fire. She was in the room with him, but he could tell she was far away mentally. She was lost somewhere in her memories of that night and what she had seen and heard.

Her eyebrows pinched together. He couldn't be sure whether she were deep in thought or in pain. He wanted nothing more than to reach into her mind and know her every thought. If he could, he would make the memories less painful for her and somehow help her arrange the jumbled pieces.

He should be happy. This was what he wanted, after all. He wanted to know the secrets only she could tell. She had been the only person in the room that night, the only person other than the true murderer, and she could prove his father's innocence. With her help, he could bring honor back to his family. His father would be free, maybe even able to take over his rightful spot as head of the Royal Guard once the throne was returned to the rightful heirs.

"Your father saved me that night." Her voice was a soft whisper.

Ronin wasn't sure if it were a question or a statement. She was just working it through in her mind. Saying it aloud could be her way of clearing the haze of memories. "He rescued me."

"Yes." There was more, so much more. But he couldn't push her. Not now when her memories were finally returning.

"Then what happened?" Thea pulled her hands back and turned to face him. "What happened to your father after that night? Is he still the head of the Royal Guard and in control of those who are trying to kill me?"

"No." He hadn't realized her mind was rushing so far ahead, piecing so many things together so quickly. He couldn't let her think that, not for a second. But could he trust her with the truth now? Could she handle it? "After that night, my father was charged with the murder of the king and imprisoned."

Now that the truth was out, he could only hope she would believe him. She had to know his father wasn't capable of such a despicable deed. The look of disbelief and dismay that showed on her face was his answer.

"Your father rescued me, then they charged him with killing my father and imprisoned him?" She moved away from the fire and turned to face him. "How does that even begin to make sense?"

It didn't make sense, not really. But it had happened. His family name had been tarnished.

It was a wonder they'd even let him continue his training in the Junior Guard before telling him they had no place in the Guard for him. His older brothers had been dismissed immediately. He could only imagine they thought him young and impressionable. They had thought wrong.

"Why didn't your father just tell them…?" Her question trailed off. Then she answered it herself as the realization dawned. "He couldn't tell them he had rescued me that night without letting everyone know I was alive. So he had no way of proving his innocence. He kept the secret even though it meant he would be imprisoned for a crime he didn't commit."

He could see how the truth hurt her. It was that genuine hurt that showed him some good had come from his father's decisions. His father had been so determined to protect the heirs to the throne, he hadn't told anyone he'd been there rescuing the princess. Without an alibi, he'd quickly become the easiest scapegoat. He'd been unable to protect himself without handing the prince and princess over to those who had tried to kill them.

Even upon threat of prison, he'd refused to jeopardize their safety.

Ronin hadn't understood it then. But now that he'd met Thea, he could see the woman she'd become and he could finally respect his father's choice. He had worried how he would ever explain to her what his father had done, but she'd figured it out all on her own.

"It's not your fault." He reached out to smooth the lines of guilt and worry from her face.

"It just doesn't make sense," she whispered, finally relaxing against him. She didn't move away this time when he brought his arms around her and held her.

"There are a lot of things in this world that don't make sense. But we have the chance to make it right." He had no words other than those to try to help erase the pain he knew she felt. He'd felt that same pain when he'd known his father had been innocent and imprisoned anyway. He'd saved the princess and then turned right around and kept saving her. He was an innocent man, yet he had given up years of his life to protect her.

"Bringing me home helps clear his name." She raised her head and looked into his eyes. Light from the fire flickered across her features. "Doesn't it?"

"It could." There would be a little more to it than Thea suddenly reappearing after all this time. It would obviously clear his father of her murder, but it still didn't explain the king's death or that of her younger sister.

"Is that the real reason you came for me?"

Her question was so heartfelt, it tore at him to give her an honest answer.

He was saved from answering the question as the lights flickered once again. Then with a pop they were out. For a moment they were surrounded by near darkness and only the light and sound of the fire. Thea stood frozen in place. He felt her stiffen and watched the play of emotions across her face. First the shock, then the fear.

Ronin drew her close. He knew her thoughts were that someone had come after them and cut the power to the house.

"It's just the storm," he said. "You're safe."

He said the words to reassure her, but he needed to make sure. The men from the woods couldn't have found them so soon...unless they hadn't turned back as they'd said and had followed him and Thea instead. Ronin eased away to a window and peered outside. The world was black with the outside lights out, as well. It seemed unlikely the power outage was caused by anything other than the storm. If the men had followed them, they didn't seem like the sort to take the time to cut the power. They'd have come in with guns blazing.

"Are you sure?" Her eyes darted around the room, searching every shadow. "Are you sure they didn't follow us?"

Sure? There weren't many things in the world that were 100 percent. "I just came in from outside. I walked the perimeter. No one is out there."

No one had been behind them all those miles they had been driving, either. It seemed almost impossible that they could have been found that quickly and easily. Neither did it seem believable that someone had followed them so doggedly through the woods. Something didn't feel quite right about it.

In the distance he could hear the couple returning. Sounds of their laughter and hollering out to each other grew closer until a faint flicker of candlelight preceded them into the room.

"Guess we didn't move quite fast enough to get back before we lost power, but we're here now. We've brought snacks and these little guys." Lizzie entered the room first with a bag of marshmallows and a candle. Her husband followed carrying a box.

"We thought you might like the extra company and they need to stay warm," he said.

With a flash Thea's features changed and

softened as she leaned over, looking into the box.

She started to reach in and then pulled her hand back. "Can I touch them?"

"Of course. They love the attention. Momma's around here somewhere, probably scared from the storm."

Thea reached in and pulled out a small, wriggly ball of skin and fur.

"They're adorable." She pulled the black-and-white puppy close, stroking it as she snuggled it against her heart. "I've always wanted a puppy."

The room grew quiet. He knew she'd never had a pet. It was one of the many facts on paper about her. But all the times he'd read the details of her life, he'd never really thought about what those little statistics had meant.

"Well, she's yours until the momma comes out of hiding. They'll need to eat then, but for now we'll fix them a nice warm place here by the fire."

"If it's okay with you two, we usually just curl up in front of the fire when the power goes out like this," Earl said.

"Sounds good," Ronin replied. Actually, the power going out was a blessing in disguise. He could keep an eye on Thea without having to park himself outside her door all night.

"I've got enough pillows and blankets here for everyone. We should have a place for each of us to relax, but someone might get a little squished in the chair or love seat."

"Anyplace is going to be fine for me." He didn't expect to get much sleep tonight anyway. He took the pillow and blanket Lizzie handed him and made a spot a few feet from the sofa, propping himself up against the wall so he could see everyone in the room along with every possible entrance.

Thea plumped up a pillow and snuggled more into the sofa, the puppy lying in the crook of her arm as she settled in. Her fingers rubbed up and down over its back as she held it close.

"I'll just move the puppy bed over near the sofa, then," Lizzie said before claiming a spot on the love seat. "And then maybe you can tell me more about how you two met and we can roast some marshmallows."

Her husband tossed a few more logs onto the fire and settled into the recliner. "I'm sure it's an interesting story."

Ronin couldn't help but chuckle. He glanced over at Thea and noticed she'd been watching him, as well. Her returning smile made him wonder what she was thinking.

"It was very interesting indeed," she pronounced. "It all started with a brick, actually."

He wasn't surprised at all with the way Thea shared. She was a genuinely open person. He had no reason to expect she'd keep the full truth from these people who had opened up their home and given them safe harbor on a night that had gone so very wrong. If not for spotting their home and being welcomed in, Ronin was not sure what he'd have done.

Thea's faith was solid. If she'd had any doubt during the night that things would not work out, she hadn't shown it. He'd caught her a few times, head bowed in prayer. Of course she'd had her moments when she'd let the fear show, but she'd never let it overtake her and rule her emotions and thoughts. He was right about her being strong. He could only hope she'd be strong enough to handle the rest of their journey and whatever truths were yet to come to light.

EIGHT

The dream was the same.

There were voices. A man and a woman arguing. She could barely make out any words but she sensed they were not happy. Father was trying to calm them. He spoke softly just like he did to her when she was upset.

She was upset now and she wished more than anything he would take her in his arms and tell her everything was okay.

She drew her knees up and hugged them close. She wanted to run out and help, to say or do something. But Poppa had said to stay. No matter what. Thea tried to pull herself into a tiny little ball, hoping it would make her invisible. There was a gasp and then a gunshot. Then another. The sound clutched at her heart. The silence after that was deafening.

She shrank as far back into the closet as she could, her hands over her mouth to keep from screaming. If they knew she was there, they would come for her next. They would kill her. She knew it. Her father had told her to stay, and she always did what he told her to do. She stayed and waited. She listened to the sounds of the man and woman outside the closet door. They were arguing again. She heard the rustle of clothing, people moving around in the room. Then the smell came, a light scent of vanilla as she heard the rustle of a dress pass by the door.

The door flew open. Someone was there. Behind the hazy silhouette she could see her father lying on the floor.

Then the fire—there was always fire.

She looked up into the face of the person she knew had killed him. But then there was always darkness.

Thea awoke with a start, bolting upright from her scrunched position on the sofa. Her hand automatically flew to her forehead and the visible reminder of how close she'd come to death that night. She'd been told afterward she'd been hit over the head with something heavy and left for dead in the fire. Thea shook the thought away.

The aroma of cinnamon and vanilla floated through the air. Her stomach gurgled. No wonder she had smells in her dream. She'd never had that before. Part of her wanted to think she'd discovered some new clue, but her rational mind could only deduce it was because of the smells in the house around her.

A log on the fire cracked, making a popping sound and sending sparks shooting onto the hearth. She looked and found the room nearly empty. Ronin sat in a chair by the fire, watching her. He was always watching her. It was unnerving.

"You're staring again." Thea ran her fingers through her hair in an attempt to straighten the mess tossing and turning all night had probably left behind.

"You were dreaming."

"You should have woken me." Thea swung her legs over the side of the couch, careful for the puppies that had fallen asleep in the box on the floor next to her.

"The puppies are outside right now," he said, noticing how she was being careful of where to put her feet. "And you needed to rest. We're going to have a long day."

"Are we leaving?"

"We need to. The longer we stay here, the more we put these people in danger." His voice was calm, his gaze steady on her.

"I agree." She didn't want to put her new friends in any more danger than they already had by staying here. "You're still staring."

"You're beautiful." The room was filled with

an awkward silence. She wasn't sure if he was being genuine or joking with her. She resisted the urge to fuss with her hair again. Despite the fact she assumed she looked a fright, a thrill shot through her. No one had ever called her beautiful. In fact, she'd always gone out of her way to downplay any beauty she might have. She'd spent her life needing to blend in, remaining in the shadows and not drawing attention to herself.

Thea had no idea what the proper response would be, so she chose to ignore it. She placed both her feet on the floor. Pain shot through her legs and body.

He noticed her grimace. "Are you in a lot of pain?"

"Only when I move," she teased. "If I get up and move around a little, I'm sure it will subside."

She studied him. The gash she had inflicted on his forehead looked better, but there were other scrapes and bruises she probably should have noticed before now. He had been through the same ordeal. He had to be pretty banged up from his air bag and the crash. He'd tried to shelter her from as much as possible.

"How are you feeling this morning?" she asked awkwardly.

"I've seen worse. I'll be fine."

Just then, the puppies came bouncing back into the room. Jumping and rolling along the hardwood floor, they half ran, half slid to their spot in the box near her feet. Yips and tiny little growls brought a smile to her face. Their fat little bellies were witness to the fact they'd eaten well recently.

The black-and-white one she had held until she'd slept waddled up to her feet and began tugging on her pant leg. She lifted it onto her lap.

"You've really never had a puppy?"

"Was that information not in my documentation?" After she spoke the words, she realized how curt they sounded. She didn't want to sound like a bitter shrew. "I'm sorry," she added.

If he noticed either her rudeness or apology, he didn't make a fuss of it.

"It was, but I thought maybe you'd like to talk about it."

"There's nothing to talk about, really. Father always said 'maybe someday.' We'd been picking out a few breeds that would work well as the royal puppy. It just never happened." Not just any dog could be the dog of the royal family, after all. It had been frustrating. She'd been a child and she'd just wanted a puppy. Any mutt off the street would have made her happy. Now the puppy jumped at her face, licking and nibbling. "Then after the fire…" Her words trailed off as she remembered back to all those moves, all those homes. It had been impossible to have a pet then. "It's not important."

She was saved from needing to answer more when Lizzie walked into the room.

"Oh, good, you're awake. The power is back and I've got breakfast in the kitchen."

"I thought I smelled something amazing." The mention of food reminded her of the smells in her dream. For a moment she wondered if she should say something to Ronin. But the more she thought about it, the more certain she was it had only been the food cooking that had made its way into her dream. It seemed silly to bring it up now.

"Pancakes. I thought it would give you a lovely start to your day."

"Let me just wash up first and I'll be right there." As she spoke Thea placed the puppy back on the floor with her brothers and sisters. Ronin rose at the same time and made to follow her out of the room. "I really think I can manage to get to the bathroom on my own."

The elderly woman chuckled. "Give her some privacy, young man, and come help me set the table."

Thea made her way up the stairs slowly. She

glanced over her shoulder to be sure he was indeed giving her some space and not following her. He watched her from his spot in front of the fire until she was out of sight.

The details of her dream floated in and out of her mind. She'd had nearly the same dream many times through the years. But this time it was different. There was something she couldn't quite put her finger on that she knew was important. Figuring it out could keep them safe when they arrived in Denver. She knew it. She would just have to keep replaying that night in her mind until she figured it out.

Her future and their safety might depend on it.

The hood of the beat-up truck fell shut with a slam.

"She isn't pretty, but she'll get you where you're going." Earl ran a gloved hand over the cracked paint on the hood. "She's only got rust holding her together in a few spots, but she's got a solid engine." The man chuckled and tossed over the keys.

"I really appreciate all your help." The man had truly gone above and beyond. Not many people would have been so accommodating to total strangers and handed over the keys to a vehicle, as well. "As soon as I get Thea to Denver, I'll see that you are repaid for your kindness."

"Didn't do it for repayment."

Ronin thought of saying more but didn't want to offend the man or his gracious offer. He wasn't sure what they'd have done without him. It would be very likely he'd have had to make that phone call to his brother Jarrod to arrange for financial assistance or help with transportation. With so many people only out to harm them, it was heartening to see there were still those with a kind heart.

"Still, I'll at least do my best to get your truck back to you in one piece."

"I know you will, son, but more important than that is keeping the princess safe and getting her home to her family."

"You can count on that." Ronin glanced outside the shed to where the truck was parked. Every now and then the sun attempted to shine through the haze of gray clouds still hovering over the countryside. As far as the eye could see into the hilly horizon, there was nothing but white. The storm had left behind at least a foot of snow and ice. Drifts where the wind had blown the snow across roads and the countryside would be even deeper.

"It seems to have let up now," Earl said, as if sensing Ronin's thoughts about the weather.

"The snowplows should start making the rounds soon."

"That's good." He didn't want to scare the old man, but if the snowplows could get through, so could other vehicles. Plowed roads cleared the way for the men who were after Thea. The longer they stayed, the more dangerous it was for everyone. He hated the thought that their trail might lead here. "When I get to town, I'll send someone back to check on you."

"No need to fret about us." The man spoke in a calm tone without a hint of worry. "The phone lines will be up again soon, and I'll make a call to the sheriff myself."

Ronin nodded. He'd make a few calls himself. The couple's kindness would not be repaid with danger. He'd see to that.

"I'm headed back in for some of that hot chocolate the wife was fixing."

"I'll be right there." Thoughts of the men coming back had his mind on once again checking the perimeter. Just in case.

As he turned the corner at the back of the shed, he was surprised by a snowball in the face. Clearing it away from his eyes, he noticed the smiling woman standing in the yard with what looked like the beginnings of a wobbly snowman.

"I'm guessing that was no accident."

"That's very astute of you," she replied, bending over to scoop up another handful of snow.

"You really shouldn't dish it out if you can't take it."

"And why would you think I can't take it?" Her question was followed by another snowball aimed directly at his head. A quick move to the side and it went flying by, missing its target.

"For starters, you have terrible aim. Not to mention your snowballs are not packed nearly tight enough. Half of it is falling apart before it gets to me."

She laughed. "It would have hit you if you hadn't moved. There's nothing wrong with my aim. But tighter snowballs, that I can do." She smiled, taking her time to gather up a larger amount of snow before packing it tightly into a nice grapefruit-sized ball.

They didn't have time for this. They should be gathering their few belongings and loading the truck so they could get on the road. But seeing her smiling and laughing was his undoing. She was happy. For the first time in the short time he'd known her, she seemed carefree. Not at all like the woman who had been distant and fearful just the day before.

These few moments of lightheartedness

might be all she'd have for a few days. If not longer. He'd be cruel to take that away from her.

"How's that for aim and consistency?" she said, shooting another snowball toward his face.

The ball hit him dead center on his chest. "Depends what you were aiming for." He laughed. Life and death were not a light matter to him. But here, in this moment with her, there were no assassins, no princess and no throne. There was just a man, a woman and snow.

She laughed again as she bent over to scoop up more snow. Her laughter touched a part of him he hadn't realized existed. The sound warmed him and temporarily made him believe in the good things in life again. It gave him hope.

Ronin stepped toward her before she could fire off another round.

"Your snowman is a little wobbly," he said, hoping to distract her while he made his own ball of snow.

"Are you ridiculing my masterpiece?" Thea asked as she began gathering more snow.

"I'm not sure what you are going for there, but if you add any more snow to the top, it's going to send it toppling over."

Thea laughed. "Toppling is definitely not

what I'm going for." She stood, hands on hips, glaring down at the rounded mess she had started. "Do you maybe have some pointers on snowman building that you'd like to share then?"

"I'm not sure this snow is good packing snow, but you're going to need a steadier foundation." Ronin packed the snow he'd gathered in tight around the base she had already started. "The trick is going to be making the bottom nice and solid before starting in on the body and head."

"It's good to know I've got the right man for the job." Thea bent down and began helping him pack the snow tighter around the base. She laughed and teased him as he explained what he thought were the proper techniques. He was just making most of it up. He'd never been much of a snowman builder. But for now she didn't have a care in the world.

That was the way it should be. She shouldn't have to live a life of always watching over her shoulder and wondering if someone was going to try to kill her. She should be safe in her castle somewhere. In a matter of days she would be. He'd get her to Denver, and once her identity was verified, she'd be well guarded. She'd be whisked away to her home in Portase. She would be safe.

"She's looking much better!" Thea exclaimed as they added a few twigs for arms.

"She?" Ronin questioned.

"Of course." She stood next to him. "Not all snowmen have to be men." For a moment she looked puzzled. "I guess that would make her a snowwoman, though."

"I guess so." Ronin looked down at her and smiled.

She stood inches away from him, her eyes filled with laughter. She dusted the scattering of snow from his shoulders and reached up to brush the already melting bits from his hair. He noticed the moment the mood changed from playful and carefree to something else.

Something different.

He looked down into her eyes and was taken aback by the emotion he saw there. Her eyes were filled with happiness and, if he didn't know better, love. She was just happy, he told himself. Nothing else.

The roar of the snowplow pulled them both from their trance.

"They're clearing the road," she whispered, not moving away from him.

Ronin was the one to pull away. He'd forgotten his place again. He'd forgotten he was here to protect her, not play games. He should know better. One moment with your guard down was all it took for someone to die. What happened with Leo had proved that fact to him. She might not have blamed him, but he blamed himself.

Even now they could be in danger. His eyes skimmed the tree-lined drive that led to the small farmhouse. The men could have followed them here and even now be waiting to make their move. It had been so easy for them to find them before. They'd followed them tenaciously. It was almost as if they were tracking... His thought trailed off as the realization finally hit him.

They were tracking them.

"Thea."

"It's time to go." Her voice was barely a whisper, filled with disappointment.

"It's not that." Yes, it was time to go, but if what he was thinking was true, there wasn't a second to waste. "Do you have anything on you? Something that you have been carrying with you all this time?"

"I've been wearing the same clothes, if that's what you mean."

"Not your clothes." He couldn't believe he hadn't thought of it sooner. The fact that he hadn't was more proof that his mind hadn't been on his job. "Something smaller. Jewelry, like a ring or locket?" All the royal family had some sort of tracking device. The king had seen to that detail when his children were young.

The devices hadn't been needed when the royal family was thought dead, so they had been deactivated. But now—now the person who had tried to eliminate them so many years ago would know they were alive. That person would go to any lengths to be sure the princess remained dead. Now was a good time for the trackers to be activated again.

An array of emotions swept over her face. First confusion, apprehension and then fear.

"I have my family medallion. My father gave it to me."

"Give it to me." That was it. It had to be. He knew she'd struggle to let go of something that obviously meant so much to her. So now more than ever, she needed his honesty.

She needed to know how important it was to get rid of it.

"They are tracking us through it, Thea. We need to destroy it."

"Destroy?" Her voice was filled with emotion as she choked the words out. "You can't. It's all I have left."

For a few seconds he wondered if he were going to have to search her and find the medallion himself. But just as he was about to move toward her, she reached into her pocket. Pulling it out, she held it in her fist in front of him.

"If we keep it, they will track us. They will find us and they will kill us." He grabbed her by the shoulders. He wanted to shake some sense into her. He was annoyed with himself for not thinking of it sooner. Frustration wasn't what she needed from him now, though. She needed assurance and comfort. He pulled her close. Her hand remained fisted between them.

"That's what the men meant when they talked about losing it, wasn't it?" Her words were muffled against his chest, but he knew she referred to the things the men had said when they'd nearly found them in the woods. He should have realized it then.

"Yes," he said. He was a fool for not figuring out how they'd tracked them. He'd let his guard down. He'd jeopardized her safety.

Ronin wrapped his arms around her and held her, giving her a few moments to come to the realization he knew she would.

"Give it to me, Thea." He moved back enough to grab her hand. His fingers wrapped around hers. "Give it to me and I will give you back more than a piece of metal. We will get through this and you will have your family back."

She pulled her hand from his and held it to her chest. Over her heart.

Her shoulders slumped and she relaxed. He held out his hand and slowly she placed the warm medallion in his palm. Bits of snow fell off her gloves, melting against the warmth of it.

A strong desire rushed through him to take her back in his arms, hold her and tell her everything was going to be all right, but he couldn't. He'd already wasted enough time.

He left her standing, walked to the shed and grabbed a sledgehammer he'd seen earlier. Thea stood near a large tree stump used for chopping wood. He walked toward her and placed the medallion on its surface, pausing for only a moment. The need to keep her safe and the desire to not hurt her warred in his mind.

"You don't have to watch." He hoped she would agree and leave him to do what must be done.

"Yes, I do," she replied.

She would be angry. She would be heartbroken. But she would be alive. He brought the heavy hammer crashing down, sending the medallion into splintered pieces between them.

"They won't be able to track us now."

She stood frozen in place. He couldn't look into her eyes. Whether she blamed him or not, he'd allowed her brother to be shot, and then he'd taken away the one material possession she had to remind her of her family.

"Now we leave?" she asked after a few minutes had ticked away.

"Yes," he said, staring down at the remnants of her life he had crushed.

"Just let me grab my bag and tell Earl and Lizzie goodbye."

Thea didn't wait for a reply. She turned away from him and walked slowly to the house. He watched her back as she moved past the snowman they had just built. She stopped. For a moment he thought she might reach out to it. But she didn't.

He had spoiled the memory of this place for her. She deserved good memories. Now he'd taken it all from her. Telling himself over and over in his mind that it had to be done for her safety couldn't erase the pain in her eyes.

At least now there would be distance between them. For a few moments he'd thought that there could be more to their relationship than him keeping her safe and getting her to Denver. He'd thought wrong. He was not the sort of man a princess could be interested in. Just like the puppy search she'd told him about. Not just any man was fit for a princess.

He was a stray. He had no pedigree or

papers. Any feelings she'd had before this moment were born from gratitude toward him and his family. She wasn't grateful now.

It was for the best. She deserved better than anything he could give her, and he definitely didn't deserve a woman as amazing as her.

NINE

They were on the road again.

She knew the medallion had only been an object. He was right to destroy it. No matter how fast or far they ran, they would always find her if they could track her that easily. She was a fool for not thinking of it sooner.

But her heart ached.

Giving it to him knowing it would be destroyed had left a tiny hole in her heart. It was all she had left of her father, of her family. As much as she knew he was right, that it had to be done, her heart still broke with the finality of it all. With it, her past was destroyed. All that lay ahead was an uncertain future.

God knew the plans He had for her. Her faith had taught her to trust even in moments of doubt. But she couldn't help but wonder if she would be in more danger once the truth of her existence was revealed. Thea focused on the passing scenery in an attempt to take her mind off the loss and uncertainty. The roads were still barely drivable. She wasn't sure if the road conditions really constituted "cleared," but this was probably as good as it was going to get until the temperatures rose enough to melt some of the ice and snow. Travel was a little faster than it had been the last time they were on the road, but not much. The plows had gotten a lot of the drifts off the roads, but there were still spots covered in packed snow and ice.

The beat-up old truck was a much bumpier ride than Ronin's car had been. Thankfully, he stuck to mostly state highways, and for the past few hours they'd traveled along an interstate. Ronin seemed secure in the thought that they wouldn't be tracked or found as easily now, but she noticed that he kept a close eye on any vehicles they came across.

She hadn't said much to him since they'd left the farmhouse. It wasn't because she blamed him. She just had so much to think through now that she'd learned more of the danger she faced. There were so many things she hadn't known, so many pieces to the puzzle of what had happened to her family. She had no idea why she hadn't thought to ask all the questions sooner. She'd only done what she was told.

Now for the first time in years she felt she

was regaining control of her life. She might not have all the answers, but she knew someone who had most of them.

"If it was that easy to track me and find me, why are they just now coming for me?"

Ronin glanced her way at the question, then quickly back at the road ahead.

"Why now?" she asked again. She reached over and turned down the music that had been playing the past few hundred miles.

"There was no need to track you when everyone thought you dead. The trackers were deactivated until recently."

"I was safe because I was dead." Thea sighed and went back to looking out the window. It was so odd to think everyone had for so long thought of her as dead. In a way she supposed she had been. She'd been hidden away, existing but not really living, for so many years. If it hadn't been for her faith and the knowledge that God had been with her through it all, she didn't know if she would have come through as the person she was now.

"Yes," Ronin replied. "Only a handful of people knew you and your brother weren't killed in the fire. When the country became restless, the truth was leaked."

"By who?" she asked.

"We don't know." Ronin's fingers tightened

around the steering wheel. "My brother Jarrod is working on it."

"What about Leo?" she asked quickly. Guilt clutched at her heart. If she had a tracker, Leo would, as well. She should have thought of him sooner. "Won't they be tracking him, too?"

"Yes." Ronin exhaled heavily. "But he is well protected, and I will make a call. He will be okay."

"Reactivating the tracking devices would have had to be done by someone of high ranking in the Royal Guard or by the king himself." Thea's mind rushed through all the possible suspects. "Who would want us dead?"

"The person who killed your father, for one. They would be worried you might remember something from that night. The king or someone who supports him, for another."

"That gives us a lot of suspects, then, doesn't it?" It seemed hopeless the person behind it all would ever be captured. "How will we ever catch whoever is behind it all?"

"*We* won't." Ronin glanced over at her. He knew what she was thinking. "Your only concern when we arrive will be what jewels to wear with what dress."

Thea squirmed in her seat. She didn't like it one bit that he could tell what she was thinking so easily. But if he thought she would just stand by and play dress up while he hunted down whoever was trying to kill her, he was wrong.

"Will Leo be in Denver?" Thea changed the subject. It wouldn't do any good to argue with him about what she would or wouldn't do on their arrival. The more she revealed of her thoughts, the more he'd know how determined she was to be a part of ensuring her father's killer was finally brought to justice. The fact that Ronin's father had been imprisoned for all these years was unfathomable. He would be freed as soon as she had the power to do so.

Leo would help her with that, she was sure. He would be just as appalled about what had happened. She couldn't wait to finally be a family with him again.

"He will be there eventually." His words were like ice water on the hope that had been building inside her.

"But you told me you would take me to Leo." Doubts assailed her. Had he only used Leo as a ploy to gain her cooperation and trust? Was she foolish in believing everything he'd told her was the truth? For all she knew Leo could be dead. It could all be a lie.

"I want to see Leo." Thea spoke the words as calmly as she could over the thudding of her racing heart.

"I told you I would take you to Leo and I

will." His abrupt answer only fueled her uncertainty. He glanced at her quickly. "It's not safe to have you both in the same place at the same time," he continued. "We have to keep you separate until the threat is eliminated."

Thea took a deep breath. She didn't like his answer, but it made sense.

"Can I at least talk to him?"

"As soon as it's possible." Ronin nodded. "You have my word."

She studied his profile. Was his word enough? She'd only known him twenty-four hours. Was she a complete fool for putting her total trust in him?

"Are you planning on stopping anytime soon?" she asked. She needed a break. Maybe distance from him, even if for only a few minutes, would clear her head. Not to mention how good getting up and walking would feel after hours of being in the car.

"There's a rest stop up ahead. I can pull over there if you like."

"I'd like that very much."

Thea went back to watching out the window and as soon as the truck pulled to a stop, she opened her door. She knew he'd be around within moments to open it for her. Doors, however, were one thing she could do on her own.

"I'll be right outside if you need me," he

shouted as she made her way to the ladies' restroom at the side of the building.

The room hadn't been cleaned recently. Cobwebs filled every corner. The lights were dim, maybe so no one would notice the grime in the toilet bowls and around the edges of the sinks and faucets. She wasn't prissy by any means, but she was afraid to touch anything.

Thea stared into the mirror, but a blurry reflection stared back. The mirrors weren't even made of glass. They were more like a polished aluminum.

Thea washed her hands quickly. The sooner she was out of here, the better.

She reached with her elbow to press the button on the hand dryer, hoping it would be in working order. The hum of the blower filled the small room. Something scurried from the shadows, making a path over her foot.

Thea shrieked, jumping back. Her eyes darted around every corner, searching for whatever it was that she'd frightened out of hiding.

She stepped back slowly, watching and waiting for it to jump out at her again.

She backed all the way to the door and then flung it open and ran straight into a hard body. She shrieked again.

"Are you okay?" Ronin asked. "I heard you scream." His voice was filled with worry.

Relief flooded her.

Foolish or not, she trusted him. He made her feel safe and protected. Even if that protection was only from small, furry creatures.

"Yes, it was just a mouse...or a rat." It could have been a large bug, actually, but a rat sounded so much more frightening, like something that would make someone scream.

"A mouse?" he questioned.

"Or a rat." She moved behind him, using his body as a shield in case the offending vermin were to follow her outside and lunge at her. "You know they carry disease. It could be rabid."

"A rabid rat?"

"Are you laughing at me?" She really didn't have to ask. She could hear the laughter in his voice. It brought a smile to her heart despite the circumstances, despite the fact that only a few moments before she had been so unsure about him. She'd been silly. He was only doing what he felt was right; deep down she knew that, even if she didn't agree with him. The sound of him being happy was something she had only heard a few times, but it brought her more joy than she thought any simple sound could bring.

"I would never do that." He was and he would, but if she could bring him any happiness by squealing like a fool at rats, then bring on the rats. It would be worth it. "If I sound at all amused, it's only because I am relieved you were not being attacked."

She turned to face him. Laughter lit his eyes. Laugh lines that she'd never noticed before creased along his lips, showcasing a small dimple on his left cheek.

"I *was* being attacked," she teased. "Only by something of the four-legged variety is all. I think I nearly jumped out of my skin."

"Maybe it's time to collect your skin and get out of here, then. Before it returns."

"That is a very good idea. It might have just gone to get friends to terrify me."

Despite their words, they stood in place looking into each other's eyes. She didn't want to be the first to move and end the moment. He didn't seem in a hurry, either. The warmth of his smile made her feel safe. He would protect her, even from rats.

He would lay his life down for her. It was that fact that frightened her more than anything else. She did not want his death on her conscience. He had come to mean a great deal to her. Even after such a short time she'd begun to wonder what her life would be like without him in it. That life was not something she wanted to imagine.

A day on the run with him had opened her eyes to many things about herself and life that she'd only imagined were possible. She'd always hoped someday she would have a home, a family. That life was something she'd prayed for nearly every night since childhood. When she was younger, that family had been her brother and her. As she got older, she'd thought it impossible to hope it might include a man. Her life had been too complicated to imagine that. But if it did, she had no doubt it would be a man like Ronin.

She was sure he had his own dreams of a future and family. Family was very important to him. The fact that he'd been so dedicated to proving his father's innocence showed that. For him to have that future, that life, he'd have to stay alive. That wasn't likely to happen if he stayed with her. Her future was uncertain. With so many out to kill her, and Ronin so determined to protect her, it was possible this might not end well.

Her thoughts only strengthened her resolve.

She would leave him. She'd nearly ditched him before. Now she was more aware of how he thought, so she could do it again. Not because she didn't trust him, but because she did.

Only this time he wouldn't know she was even gone until it was too late.

Thea turned away from him. Instantly she missed his smile, his warmth. Her heart sank as she followed Ronin back to the truck, but with the decision made, she knew it was for the best.

Back on the road she kept her eyes averted out the window. If he looked into her eyes there was a chance he'd see what she was thinking and she couldn't have that. She had to stay focused on what she needed to do. She wasn't sure when or where she'd make a run for it, but she'd stay alert and ready. He would be angry and he would do his best to find her, but maybe she could keep him off track just long enough to find her brother and get home.

She was tired of running.

It was time to turn the tables and become something other than the hunted.

It was time for her to become the hunter.

She was up to something. Ronin wasn't sure what, but something had changed since the rest stop. After he'd rescued her from the rat, she seemed different. Gone was the soft woman he'd spent the day traveling with and protecting. In her place was the hardened fighter he'd met that first night.

It was surprising that he could read her so well after such a short time. He didn't even have to look into her eyes to see that she was deep in thought about something that he wouldn't like. She'd been tense and her breathing had changed. She was watching the road signs even more intently than he was. If he didn't know better he'd say she was afraid. She couldn't be afraid of him; they had moved past that.

Or he thought they had.

Granted, he hadn't given her many reasons to trust him when he'd kept so much from her.

"Any good snacks left?" he asked in an attempt to get her talking again. At least then he'd have a chance to try to sort out what was going on in her mind.

Thea turned toward him, rummaging through the bag of snacks Lizzie had packed for their journey.

"Do you think they'll be okay?" she asked, her voice a whisper of worry.

"Yes." He didn't have to ask who she meant. The elderly couple had been on his mind, as well. "Earl knows how to take care of himself, and we'll make a call at the next town."

Ronin breathed a sigh of relief. Worry over the people who had taken them in explained Thea's change in behavior. He should have alerted the authorities by now, but his first priority was Thea. Earl could take care of his family.

"How hungry are you?" Thea asked. "There are a couple sandwiches still in here, some potato chips and cookies."

"Homemade?" he asked. He'd never been one to turn down homemade cookies.

"Looks that way." Thea pulled out a small ziplock bag, inspecting it closely. "Peanut butter."

"Sounds good."

"For you," Thea remarked. "Nuts are off my menu, in case you've forgotten." Thea handed the ziplock bag over to him and closed the sack.

"There has to be something else in there you can eat."

"I'm not really hungry right now," she stated, turning her head to look back out the window at the passing countryside.

"Do you need to nap?"

"The last time I did, it did not end well."

Ronin laughed. She was right. As much as he wanted to promise her that this time would be different, he couldn't. He'd kept a close watch on the road behind them and around them, just in case. He hadn't seen anything out of the ordinary. With the tracker destroyed, they should be impossible to find. They might actually be able to make it the rest of the way to Denver without any further problems.

That might only be a sign of the worst yet to come, though. If the men weren't out looking for them, then that could only mean they were waiting and ready for their arrival. Getting her to the safe house his brother should have set up wouldn't be a problem. After that, things could get dicey. There was no real way to tell just how her return would be accepted.

He didn't like going in blind. He needed to call and make sure that everything was ready as they'd planned before they walked right into a trap.

Making a phone call might be just what they were waiting for. But he'd be smart about it. According to the signs, a city was up ahead. It was big enough to have a store where he could purchase a disposable phone. He'd make a quick call and then get rid of the phone before anyone had a chance to track them.

If they kept up at this pace, they would make it to Denver by evening. They could stop for the night, but he doubted either one of them would be able to sleep.

Arriving under the cover of night would

work in their favor, but first he had to find out what they were arriving to.

"I'm going to stop up ahead and make that call."

Thea perked up at his words, giving him her full attention. He'd have to keep an even closer eye on her. The brilliant mind of hers was a dangerous thing when she used it against him. He still hadn't completely shaken the feeling that she was up to something. Thea up to something wasn't going to be something he'd like.

TEN

Now was her chance.

Thea saw the opportunity and she took it. Ronin would be angry. The sort of angry she hoped she wouldn't have to actually be a witness to, but he'd get over it and he'd be alive. Of course he'd come after her, but *after* her wasn't the same as *with* her. She was their main target, not him.

She was smart enough to know she'd never be able to get away from Ronin on her own, so she'd watched and waited for the perfect opportunity and the perfect person who could inadvertently help her.

"Officer," she whispered as she walked up to the police officer who had just entered the convenience store where they'd stopped.

"Yes?"

"That man," she said, pointing in Ronin's direction. A twinge of guilt shot through her, but she dismissed it. "That man has a gun. I noticed it when I brushed past him."

That much was true. She had noticed it when she'd brushed against him. Not recently, but she knew it was there. He wasn't going to leave it anywhere while she was in danger.

"Did he threaten you with it?" the officer asked quickly, his hand hovering over his own holstered weapon. Thea leaned around the uniformed man to see if Ronin had noticed her speaking with the officer. She didn't want to bring him any added trouble. He was probably already going to be in enough. "No. I just thought you should know."

"Thank you, ma'am. You should move away, get a safe distance." As he spoke, he slowly edged toward Ronin. It was then that Ronin looked up. His eyes darted between her and the officer, who had closed the distance and was nearly beside him.

He knew.

Thea backed slowly toward the entrance, unsure whether Ronin would hurt the man and come after her or take the time to try to explain why he had a gun on him. She was counting on the latter.

She'd seen a trucker leave the store only moments before and she was hoping she could get a ride. A quick glance back confirmed Ronin's hands were in the air and he was speaking. Probably identifying himself and trying to explain the situation. He would have whatever papers he needed, she was sure. Or he'd be able to make a few calls and prove who he was. He would be okay.

A bell above the door dinged as she made her escape. A blast of cold air hit her at the same time she heard Ronin hollering for her to stop. She didn't dare turn around and she definitely wasn't stopping. If Ronin went with her all the way to Denver, there was a very good chance he would die. She wouldn't put him in that sort of danger. If he had to spend a few hours or a night at a police station, at least he'd be safe.

Chilled winter wind blew against her as she ran through the parking lot, catching up to the trucker, who had already begun to pull away. She jumped up onto the foot step of the cab and beat on the window. Within seconds the window lowered.

"I need a ride," she stated. Second and third thoughts assailed her. Hopping in a vehicle with someone she didn't know wasn't one of the smartest things she'd ever done. But it also wasn't the first time she'd done it given the fact Ronin had been a stranger, as well. It had worked out well with him, so she prayed it would work out this time, too.

"Sure, hon. Where are you headed?"

"I need to get to Denver, but anywhere other than here is fine," she supplied.

She opened the door and climbed up into the cab, slamming the door behind her. For now it didn't matter where she went. She just needed to put as much time and distance between her and Ronin as she could.

"Just push the stuff out of your way," he said as she settled into the passenger seat. The space at her feet was taken up by a case of water. "Just prop your feet up on the water if it's not too uncomfortable for you. I'm headed to Denver. You're welcome to ride along."

"Sounds perfect!" She wasn't at all sure it was perfect, but it would do. She was leaving perfection behind. Six foot something of angry man was as close to perfect as she might ever get. Not that she liked Ronin angry, but she had brought it on herself. Any emotion he might show was better than none at all, she reasoned. Emotion meant there was some feeling there. He cared, even if it was only because she was his job.

The reminder of how he felt about her quenched some of the guilt she was feeling. Hopefully, the officer wouldn't hurt him, or the other way around. Ronin would see it was for the best. If his only concern was completing his job and getting her to Denver, she could do that herself.

"Do you happen to have a phone I could use?"

"Sure thing, little lady. Unlimited, so talk all you want," the stocky man said as he handed over his cell phone.

"Thank you, but I'll keep it short, I promise."

The driver pulled the truck out onto the highway. Soon, the convenience store and Ronin were only a speck of light in the distance.

Thea held tight to the phone. Her hands shook. She finally had the means to contact the outside world, but she had no idea who to call. The only number she had for her brother was the one she'd used for contact last month. He'd probably already tossed the phone or it was in the hands of the enemy. It was a chance she had to take.

Thea pushed in the numbers she knew from memory, then listened to the rings. The moments drew out as each ring signaled she could be closer to her family or even deeper in danger.

"Hello?" a voice on the other end answered.

But it wasn't her brother. Her heart hammered in her chest. She should hang up. She knew it. Tingles of fear shot up her spine.

"Who are you?" she questioned, unsure whether she really wanted to know the answer. "What have you done with my brother?"

Thea turned toward the door, keeping her voice low. She had never felt more alone and frightened than she did in this moment. She could hear breathing on the other end of the line, breathing and then muffled sounds as if someone had put their hand over the phone. She had left Ronin behind for this.

Thea stomped down the panic. She could do this. She had to do this to keep Ronin from getting himself killed.

"I have your brother here. Just stay on the line."

They were lying. She knew it as sure as she knew she'd made a mistake in thinking she could just pick up the phone and call her brother. She should never have called the number to begin with. But she had to try.

"I know you are trying to track me," she whispered into the phone in hopes she wouldn't alert the truck driver to the trouble she was in. "Just put my brother on the phone if he is there. If not, I'm hanging up."

Thea waited. She'd give him to the count of

five, then she'd disconnect. She might not be a superspy like Ronin, but she'd watched enough police shows on TV to know what was happening. She was a fool for thinking it would be as easy as a phone call.

She could hear muffled talking and then a voice came over the phone. "If you want to see your brother, come to this address." Thea quickly asked the truck driver for a pen and paper and took down the address before disconnecting the call.

She knew it was a trap. But if there was any chance at all that her brother really was there, she had to find out. Ronin had said her brother was safe. But if he were, how were they using his number? She couldn't leave him in possible danger and do nothing.

Thea handed the phone back to the man and thanked him.

"Is everything all right?" he asked.

"Yes." Thea choked on the words. Ronin was always asking her that question. "Everything is fine." But deep down she knew everything was about as far from fine as it was ever going to get. She needed help. She needed Ronin.

Ronin paced the small holding room the officer had left him in while he'd gone to check his identity. For the first time since he'd learned

Thea was alive, he was truly afraid. Not because without her he may never have the proof he needed to free his father, but because she was off on her own and in danger. She could be about to be killed and he couldn't do a thing about it. Not without knowing where she was.

He didn't have time to think about why that bothered him so much. He only knew the infuriating, stubborn woman she was had, in the short time he'd known her, crawled under his skin. She had come to mean more to him than just a way to clear his father's name. Sometime in the past few days he'd grown to admire her, maybe even care for her a little.

Maybe if he was being 100 percent honest, it had happened sooner. In the time he'd been studying her, he'd gotten to know things about her that might have otherwise taken him years. Everything he'd learned about her, he'd liked. Meeting the actual woman was the icing on the cake. She had proven herself to be everything he had imagined she would be.

He cared for her. More than he should.

Time ticked away and with every second his irritation grew. He blamed himself mostly. He'd known she was up to something. He'd thought it several times after the rat mishap. But he hadn't done anything about it. Not that there was anything he could have done other than tie her to his side.

He checked the time again. With every minute she was getting farther and farther away. Frustration seared through him. She'd been too quiet. Quiet was never a good thing when it came to Thea. Her mind was always working. It was one of the many things he'd admire about her if it weren't for the simple fact that she'd used that thinking against him.

To find her, he'd have to break his silence. He'd planned on making the call anyway, but now it would have to be to admit he'd failed. He'd lost her. She could be anywhere by now. He'd only seen enough to know she'd gotten a ride from a trucker. He'd watched the taillights disappear off into the distance. The truck was headed west, but that could have changed.

He pushed his fingers through his hair and took a deep breath, staring into what he knew was a two-way mirror. His papers would check out and someone would be in here soon to release him. By that time she could be halfway to wherever she was headed. Ronin ticked off her possible destinations in his mind. The way he saw it, she would either make it the rest of the way to Denver on her own, or she'd go in search of her brother.

Neither option was really a good idea.

The door opened and the officer who had brought him in entered. "I'm sorry to have detained you," he said, handing over Ronin's belongings. "Everything checks out. You're free to go."

Ronin bit back the bad-mannered remark that popped into his head. It wouldn't do any good to take his frustration out on the man who had only been doing his job. Afraid he wouldn't be able to say anything without showing his irritation, he merely nodded.

"Can I give you a ride back to your car?" the officer asked.

"That would be nice." Ronin followed along behind the man and within minutes he was seated back at the wheel of his loaner truck.

Ronin ripped open the package that contained the phone he'd purchased. That call now would be rather after the fact. Numerous calls had probably already been made to check out his story. He was just thankful that Jarrod corroborated his identity and backed him in whatever way was needed.

A quick phone call to thank him and see if there was a way available to get him to Denver faster was still in order. Minutes wasted away as he went through the tedious process of phone setup. With a little more force than necessary, he punched in the digits of his brother's phone and waited.

"Parrish here."

"It's Ronin. I've lost her."

He waited for his brother to lay into him about his carelessness or lack of responsibility. Instead there was silence.

"I know."

"How?" he asked.

"She made a call to her brother's old number. My source says it was intercepted by Henry Kross."

"How could they have done that?" he asked.

"We've found our leak. It was one of the men with Leo. They have his phone."

Ronin took a deep breath to keep from lashing out at his brother. That meant Thea was in danger. Even more danger than she knew. Henry was the current head of the Royal Guard. If he'd intercepted her call, the element of surprise was no longer on their side. They not only knew she was coming—they were giving her directions.

"What other information did your source have?"

Ronin was thankful they had sources. They'd be flying blind without them. It was a very good thing they'd managed to keep contacts and friends within the Guard—those who did their jobs and were respectful of the current rule but who still held fidelity to Thea's father. They would be loyal to Thea and Leo as well but only after they were brought forth and officially identified as the long-lost prince and princess.

"They gave her an address in Denver and told her to be there if she wanted to see her brother," Jarrod answered.

Ronin clenched the phone tight. Every ounce of him wanted to throw it across the truck and let go of the frustration coursing through him. He'd hoped they'd have told her something bizarre that she would have seen through in a second. She could still be safe. But hearing the words, he knew it was the one trap she'd fall for, even if she saw through it and knew her brother wasn't there. If there was even a shred of hope that Leo would be there, she'd go. Her brother was her weakness.

This very second she was headed into a trap.

"Any chance you can get me something faster than a beat-up truck?" he asked his brother. Jarrod would probably have to pull in some huge favors, but it would be worth it.

He had to beat Thea to Denver or at the very least get there when she did.

"Hold on," Jarrod said before the line went quiet.

Ronin took a deep breath and tried not to think of the possible danger Thea was already in just from getting into the truck with a stranger. He hated thinking of her being on the road without him. She was strong and stubborn, but she'd be afraid.

"I can get you on a private flight out of Hays."

Ronin checked his watch.

"I'll be there in thirty minutes." Ronin turned the key in the ignition. Dangerous road conditions or not, he'd make it. "You already have someone going to the address they gave, don't you?" He didn't have to ask to know his brother would have already dispatched someone. Jarrod was just as determined as he was to protect the princess. But he had to be sure Thea wouldn't be alone if he didn't make it in time.

"Yes," Jarrod answered. "But hurry."

Ronin disconnected the call and accelerated at dangerous speeds, steering back onto the interstate. He no longer needed to worry about staying hidden and remaining inconspicuous.

In fact, the more attention he drew to himself, the better. If they were busy watching him, then it might draw some of the attention away from Thea.

He had a princess to save, whether she wanted saving or not.

ELEVEN

It was a trap.

Deep inside Thea knew she was about to become one of those Hollywood starlets who opened the door to the psychopath even though every moment up to that point had shown it wasn't the smart thing to do. At least she was trying to be smart about it. She'd stood just outside the towering stone wall of the Denver mansion for the past half hour or so, watching people dressed in formal wear emerging from limos at the front door. She'd seen enough to know there was a party or event of some sort going on.

It didn't seem like the sort of place a person would choose to kill someone. Neither was it the sort of place her brother would be. Or she didn't think so. For the first time she stopped to think about how little she really did know about Leo. They'd only met once a year for the past few years, when they'd gotten old enough to get away on their own. Before that, they'd had very little contact. He could have changed.

She pushed the thought away. Leo was her brother. They were not the same person with the same personality, but she knew him. He was just as Ronin had described him. He hadn't changed so much that he'd have anything to do with hurting or entrapping her. She was sure of it.

From her spot across the street, she watched the caterers entering through a door at the back. Seeing an opportunity, she slowly made her way around to where they'd parked their van.

Her would-be killers probably expected her to march right through the front door and announce herself, demanding to see her brother. They thought wrong. Waiting for just the right moment, she slipped inside the back door when no one was looking. Once inside, she found a server uniform and a quiet spot to put it on quickly.

Thea grabbed a tray loaded with a mix of cucumber snacks and cheeses and moved in and out of the guests, trying to blend in with the other servers. She made her way into the main room. Music filled the air from a small string quartet that had set up in a corner. People mingled and chatted. Every now and then, someone would take an appetizer from her tray, reminding her of her subterfuge.

It was all too easy to identify the men who were security as the brooding, buff men with earpieces. She wasn't sure at this point if they were here to kill her or protect her. If they were Royal Guard, she should stay as far away from them as she could. She lowered her head, avoiding eye contact as she steered clear of them.

She knew there was a very good chance they'd used her brother to lure her here. Ronin had told her the plan was to keep them as far apart as possible, after all. But there was still a slim possibility Leo was here somewhere. She couldn't take the chance. If he was in this house, he was in danger and needed her help. She couldn't walk away.

Thea moved around the edges of the room, trying to remain as inconspicuous as possible while checking every room. She kept her eyes lowered to refrain from making eye contact. If they didn't recognize her, they would see it in her eyes. The fear.

Slowly and carefully, Thea checked every inch of the main floor. Room after room turned up nothing but lavishly dressed people chatting and eating. She wasn't sure what she was looking for. It wasn't likely they'd put a sign up for her. The main floor was clear, not a sign of her brother anywhere. Neither was there a clear sign of anyone actually looking for her. That left her with the decision of whether to go up or down. Down seemed like the logical place someone would keep a person against their will.

Weaving back toward the kitchen, Thea found a door to the cellar.

She lay her tray on the countertop and pulled at the heavy wood door. It creaked as she opened it slowly. Thea glanced around her quickly to make sure no one had noticed her, then slipped inside. The entry to the cellar started with a small hallway before the stairs descended. She waited a moment for her eyes to adjust, then closed the door behind her.

The partygoers' voices turned into muffled chatter as she made her way down the narrow staircase.

The stairs creaked with each step.

A chill raced up her spine as a shadowed figure darted from one side of the room to the other ahead of her.

"Hello?" she whispered through the tightening in her throat. She stood still after stepping from the last stair, searching the darkness for more movement or sound.

The sound of rustling jerked her attention

quickly to one side. She convinced herself it was just another rat. Just a very, very large rat. Even as she mumbled the words under her breath, she took a step backward. Then another. The last step backed her right up against a hard form.

"No rat," a gravelly male voice spoke from behind her.

Thea gasped as a strong hand covered her face, holding a cloth up against her nose and mouth. She recognized the voice from the woods. It was one of the men who had run them off the road. She kicked and hit at the man, but it was too late. She gasped for air, inhaling a pungently sweet scent. Sparks of light flashed behind her eyelids as she struggled to keep them open. They felt heavy. She felt heavy. Thea fought the blackness that threatened, all the while stumbling against the dark form. Her feet dragged along the floor as the man moved her through the darkened cellar.

"We can't take her back up through the house?" she heard another voice, this one less threatening and younger, say. "Why isn't she out yet? Isn't that stuff supposed to knock her out?"

Dizziness threatened, but she fought against it. Her world went into complete darkness when the man behind her threw something over her head. She fought against the hands holding her. She kicked out with her feet wildly, not knowing for sure what she was kicking at but knowing she had to fight.

Every movement felt sluggish; her body moved in slow motion. Even her thoughts were slowing. Then hands moved into the hood and over her mouth, stuffing cloth inside. She gagged against the foul smell and taste.

"Let's just kill her and be done with it," the younger voice suggested.

"Are you dense?" the older voice replied. "Not here—he's right upstairs. There can't be any trail that leads back to him."

She fought the nausea and darkness that threatened. There were two of them. If she could just stay focused on every little detail, it would help her escape.

"We'll have to go out the back, then," the younger voice stated.

The older-sounding man replied with a few choice words as her mind blurred. She struggled to focus, to note every detail of what they were saying.

She couldn't give up hope that if she stayed alert, she'd find a way to get free. If only she didn't feel so light-headed. Her body went limp. She struggled to get her feet back under her and stand, but she had no strength left. She could do nothing to fight them as they dragged her across the room. Her shins knocked against steps as her body was tugged upward.

The lower half of her body thumped against every step, but she felt no pain. A door creaked open and cool air flitted across her exposed skin. She wished for a small amount of fresh air to make its way up under whatever they had thrown over her head. She could barely breathe. Each gulp of air only brought in more of the foul smell.

She heard scuffling and fell to the ground as the men dropped her. The sounds of grunts and flesh and bone hitting against flesh and bone made its way through her muddled mind.

Gunshots blasted. Then men yelling.

Someone was rescuing her. Ronin. He was her last coherent thought before her world went completely black.

He had barely made it to her in time.

Ronin rushed the men coming up out of the cellar. When he spotted the limp body between them, fear like he'd never experienced welled up inside him. He smashed the grip of his gun down hard against one of the men's heads, knocking him unconscious before raising it quickly to point it at the other.

"Don't even think it." The man lifted Thea's

limp body up against him, using her as a shield. "Make one more move and the lady gets it."

"How do I know she's not already dead?" he asked. The thought made his throat tighten, but he pushed the words through. He had to remain calm and think positive thoughts. She couldn't be dead.

"I guess you're just going to have to take my word for that," the man replied. "Is it a chance you want to take?"

His need to protect Thea warred with the strong need to see the man pay for the pain he'd already caused her. He kept his gun targeted on the man's forehead. Even in the dimly lit driveway, at this distance there was no way he'd miss. But it was just as likely that the man's reflexes would pull his own trigger, killing Thea even as he fell to his own death.

Ronin couldn't take that chance. He lifted his hands in the air, holding his gun up in surrender.

"Okay, okay," he relented. "Just move the gun away from her."

"You'd like that, wouldn't you?" The man waved the gun at Thea's head as he barked out the questions. "Do you think I'm an idiot?"

Yes, he did, but under the circumstances it wouldn't be wise to tell the man so. He was saved from making any sort of reply by the sound of screeching tires and voices from the street in the front of the house. Flashes of light came around the corner of the building. Jarrod had arrived with backup.

"Tell your men to stay back," the man ordered.

"Stay back," Ronin shouted without taking his eyes off the man. "He has Thea."

He could only assume they'd done as asked when the man barked more orders.

"Open the back of the van! Quick or she gets it."

Ronin did as he was asked. He moved carefully, all the while watching the man out of the corner of his eye.

"Now get in there and put these on," the man ordered, tossing Ronin a pair of cuffs. Ronin obeyed. "Fasten them around the pole and your wrists. No funny stuff." The man came up beside him and snapped the cuffs tighter. At least he would be with her. He was glad the man had come up with that idea on his own because there was no way he was letting him leave here with Thea without him.

As soon as Ronin was fastened in to the man's satisfaction, he tossed Thea in beside him. Then he slammed the back door shut and rushed around to the driver's side.

The van roared to life and took off in a lurch.

Ronin didn't have to see out the back windows to know his brother would take care of the unconscious man who'd been left behind and tail just far enough behind the getaway vehicle to not risk endangering Thea more. Ronin had no doubts about his brother's ability to do his job well. It was Thea's limp body that worried him.

He wouldn't allow himself to think that her lack of movement was anything more than unconsciousness. The vehicle sped along, making several sharp turns along its journey. Ronin pulled against the cuffs until he could feel them cutting into his skin. It was no use.

The van stopped. Ronin couldn't make out where or why, but he was thankful the brief pause in movement gave him a chance to listen closely. He could hear her breathing. Relief soared through him. She was alive.

The van lurched ahead again. The sudden movement sent tools and pipes rolling around the floor and bumping up against Thea's still body.

"Thea," Ronin whispered, hoping to wake her enough to find out if she was injured.

"Quiet back there!" the man yelled. Ronin couldn't make out much of what he said after that. There was quite a bit of grumbling and words that didn't bear repeating.

Ronin tuned the man out and listened for sounds Thea might make if she woke. He just needed to know she was okay. That was all that mattered to him. He didn't care if he never got the details of what happened the night her father had died, or if she knew anything at all. He didn't want to see her hurt or in pain.

He wanted to save her from all that he could.

Ronin maneuvered into a position where he could reach out with his foot and nudge her. He gently rubbed the toe of his shoe against her legs, trying to see if he could prod her back into consciousness. He stopped and watched for any signs of movement. He didn't take the time to think of why he was so desperate to know she was okay; he just knew he would never be able to live with himself if she was hurt.

A buzzing of a cell phone from the front of the van startled him. He listened as the driver answered.

"Hello." The driver pulled the van over to a stop again. "Yes," he replied. Then silence. Ronin wiggled his foot against Thea again. He was rewarded with muffled choking sounds. Her body moved against his feet, her untethered hand feeling around on the dirty floor. She was alive. But she needed air.

"Yes, I understand," the man said again before disconnecting and glancing back at them.

"She needs air," Ronin said. "She needs air or she won't be able to breathe."

The man opened his door and within moments was behind the van opening the back doors. Streetlights illuminated the darkened vehicle.

"In a moment that won't be a problem," he said. The man reached into his coat pocket and pulled out a gun. "I admired your father, Princess. He was a good man, and in his honor I will make your death quick and painless."

Ronin tugged harder against his cuffs, ripping his skin. He could not sit here helplessly and watch the man kill Thea.

"To you, however, I make no such promises." The man lifted his gun, bringing the grip down hard against Ronin's forehead. "That I believe I owed you." Then he came down hard again, across his jaw. "That was just for fun."

"At least take the hood off her head so she can breathe," Ronin said, spitting out the blood that ran from his mouth.

"I would rather not look into her eyes when I pull the trigger." The man reached out and pulled Thea up into a sitting position.

Ronin knew what the man didn't. Thea was not a woman to underestimate. He'd noticed her hand moving slowly toward the steel pipe that had rolled against her during the ride. He smiled as she sprang to life when the man lifted her, her arm with the pipe swinging wildly. Even after she'd made contact with the man's head and he fell to the ground, she kept swinging.

Over and over again she swung the pipe in front of her.

"Thea!" Ronin shouted. "You got him—you can stop."

She stopped and pulled the hood away from her head. She glanced wide-eyed first at him and then to the man on the ground.

She turned to Ronin and smiled weakly. He watched the fear, the terror and the shock of what had just happened and of what she'd done register across her features. Her hair flew wildly around her face as she looked down at the man.

"It's okay. He's not getting back up anytime soon."

"Are you sure?"

"Yes." He would be more sure when he had the cuffs off and was able to use them on their assailant. "Can you get me his gun?" He knew she wasn't going to like going anywhere near the man, but he needed more from her. "And can you search him and find the keys?" He pulled at his cuffs.

A new emotion crossed her face, and for a split second he knew she was thinking of leaving him there and running again. He hoped she wouldn't. She might not want to admit yet how much she needed him, but tonight had shown him something he'd never imagined possible.

He needed her.

The terrified look left her face and she attempted a small smile.

"Bad guys really do need to learn not to talk so much," she said.

Her words surprised him.

She needed to talk to calm her nerves, he imagined. He willed her to keep moving forward and get the keys. If conversation was what she needed, he was happy to help.

"How so?" he asked.

"They always seem to make the same mistake—all that talking when they should just be getting the job done." She poked at the man and jumped back, as if she were expecting him to wake up and lunge at her. "They should just kill a person right away and get it over with instead of talking and giving the person a chance to get away."

"I guess he learned his lesson."

"Yes, yes, he did." She studied the man and

then quickly rummaged through his pockets. After a few seconds she hopped over the body. "I think I rescued you this time." With a smile of victory, she dangled the key in front of her.

Her smile warmed his heart. She was truly special and whether she was a princess or not, he needed her. Not just for the truths she held in her mind, but for who she was.

"But I wouldn't have needed rescuing at all if I hadn't had to rescue you."

"I'm sorry." Her smile vanished and he wished more than anything he could bring it back. "They told me Leo would be there. I couldn't risk it."

"I know." He understood. It still stung that she thought she would be better off without him. But he was sure she had her reasons. In the same circumstances he'd probably have done the same thing.

"Is Leo safe?" she asked. Her voice was filled with concern and a dash of fear.

"Yes." He was glad he could bring her good news among all the bad that had happened tonight. "My brother Declan is with him. He will be released from the hospital in a few days and taken someplace safe until the threat is eliminated."

"Thank you." Her smile was back and it lit

her face. "Would you still like to be rescued?" Thea teased, shaking the keys at him again.

"I would very much like to be rescued, Princess," he teased right back. "Before the cavalry arrives, if you don't mind."

"Do we have cavalry arriving soon?" she asked. Her smile faded as she moved closer to unlock the cuffs from his bloodied wrists. "You're hurt."

"So are you." She would definitely need to be checked by a doctor. He'd seen firsthand the callous way the men had treated her. There was no telling how long she'd been unconscious or how they'd knocked her out. "And yes, we do have backup this time. My brother should be here at any moment with his men."

As if on cue, three dark cars pulled in behind them in the vacant lot. He recognized his brother immediately as he emerged from the lead vehicle and strode toward them.

"Princess Dorthea, we need to get you away from here quickly."

His brother was never one to beat around the bush, but he knew Thea would only balk at being ordered without any sort of explanation.

"This is my brother Jarrod," Ronin explained. Then he asked, "Do you have the safe house ready?"

"Everything is prepared. But we need to go

now." As Jarrod spoke, his men were already moving about, picking up the still-unconscious man off the ground and securing the van. "We don't have long before the police arrive or whoever he was working for comes to finish the job."

Ronin nodded. It was imperative Thea was secure before anyone else arrived on the scene. He reached out his hand toward her and without hesitation she took it.

"Did you get the other man?" Ronin asked.

"Yes," his brother replied as they walked to the car.

"What was going on at the house?"

"It appeared to be a gathering of a select few Portasean officials." Jarrod stopped at the car, holding the door open for Thea.

"Someone else was there." Thea startled them both with the comment. "I remember them saying something about not killing…" Her voice trailed off. Ronin could only imagine the struggle it was to relive the ordeal she had just been through. "One of them wanted to kill me there and the other said something about they couldn't because *he* was there."

"He?" Ronin asked.

Thea nodded before climbing inside the vehicle.

"I'll get someone to review the guest list

right away," Jarrod stated as he started to push the door closed behind her.

"I'm with her," Ronin said, blocking the door before it could close. His tone left no room for questions. "I'm not leaving her side until we are 1,000 percent sure she's safe."

If Jarrod had a problem with it he didn't say anything as Ronin slid into the backseat next to Thea.

It was hard to believe just hours ago he'd thought he needed to distance himself. He couldn't imagine leaving her alone now. Now was when she needed him most. The danger was very real and imminent. If the killer wanted her dead before she could be presented as Princess Dorthea Jamison of Portase, they would have to do it soon.

"Is there even such a thing as 1,000 percent?" she questioned as the car started moving.

"Probably not," he said, taking her hand again. "I just want you to feel safe." Truth be told, 100 percent was complete and as safe as she could be, but when he was with her he felt whole. She was above and beyond what could complete him.

He wished it were possible to be with her after his job was finished, but it wasn't. She was about to get a dose of what her real life would be. That was a world he couldn't be a part of. Not in any capacity other than her bodyguard.

He couldn't imagine the pain it would bring to see her every day and have her be just out of reach. To see her and know what an amazing woman she was but to not be able to be a part of her life would be unbearable.

He'd rescued her and kept her safe. He would continue to do everything he could to protect her. But soon he was going to have to find the strength to say goodbye and let her go rule her land and take her throne.

That was her life, and he couldn't be a part of it.

TWELVE

Thea twirled in front of the full-length mirror. The intricate beading on her dress glimmered as it caught the sunlight beaming in through the window of the home that had been secured as a safe house. Tonight she would be presented as the long-lost Princess Dorthea Elizabeth Jamison of Portase.

Ronin had stuck by her side like glue the past few days. He'd been with her as she had been brought to the safe house his brother had set up and shown to a lush private suite. There she'd been seen by a physician to make sure she hadn't suffered any ill effects from the chemicals they'd used to knock her unconscious.

Once her health had been cleared, she'd been left alone to rest. Every time she closed her eyes, though, she heard the voices and felt the bag over her head once again. She should have felt safe knowing Ronin was on guard outside her door. But she didn't.

The days passed by in a whirlwind. She was poked and examined and felt as if she was under a microscope. But she never felt completely safe. Ronin and other guards had always been there, serving as a reminder that she was being watched. They only succeeded in reminding her that if they were watching, others, who meant her harm, could be watching, as well.

Private agencies that dealt with genetic and fingerprint testing had been brought in to once and for all confirm her identity. She'd been photographed, fingerprinted and DNA sampled to verify she was, indeed, Princess Dorthea. Ronin had barely spoken to her, but he'd always been there, blending into the background like the other guards they'd placed in her suite and at the doors. He'd made good on his promise to never leave her side, but somehow he'd managed to distance himself at the same time.

She didn't like it. Someone was still out there who wanted her dead and she wanted Ronin by her side the way he had been. She felt safe knowing he was watching, but she wanted to talk to him and be kept in the loop.

The not knowing terrified her the most. But they'd given her very little time to worry over it or do anything about it.

After her identity had been verified, she'd been pampered, coddled and treated like the princess she was supposed to be. Not that Ronin hadn't treated her well before, but it was different now.

Her hair, nails and makeup had been done to perfection. She had been provided a private assistant who saw to her every need before she was even aware she had the need. She was stuck between a world of her every dream coming true and some sort of fantasy she'd never imagined.

She barely recognized herself.

The dress was nice, though.

She twirled one more time.

Despite the glamour, she would trade it all in a heartbeat to be back in that small Kansas farmhouse, cuddled in front of a fire, her lap filled with puppies and a man seated beside her who cared for her. That was her dream. Not this.

"The color is perfect for you," Rita, her new personal stylist, complimented. Thea nodded. She was happy the woman finally didn't bow and curtsy with every word she spoke. She'd found out Rita was the sister of one of the men who worked for Ronin's brother and now they were chatting like old friends. Or what she'd imagined friends would be like. "And it will go perfectly with the emeralds in your tiara, necklace and earrings."

"It will definitely have me looking the part," Thea surmised. No matter how much they worked at dressing up her outside, she felt like an imposter. She'd left the life of a princess behind a long time ago. She hadn't known what she was giving up then. But she'd grown accustomed to a life other than royalty. She'd traded tiaras and gowns for baseball caps and denim.

She ran her fingers slowly over the detailed beading of the gown. All of this was not her. Not anymore.

"You look ready to meet the king."

The other woman's words did nothing to make her feel more comfortable. They only reminded her of the danger she was in.

"When will I meet him?" Thea asked.

"He's sent word that he will be at the dinner party tonight and that he's anxious to see you."

Thea's thoughts ran rampant. Would he try to kill her during the main course, or wait for dessert? She took a deep breath and exhaled slowly in an attempt to steady her nerves.

"All that is missing is your scent," Rita announced. "I have several here for you to choose from. We have to find just the right combination that will be uniquely yours." The woman moved to the dresser, where she had left a silver tray with various bottles, and returned with one in hand. "Just a spritz." She spoke as she sprayed a fog of perfume over Thea. "What do you think?" A light scent of jasmine and cinnamon filled the air, landing on Thea's skin with a cool blush.

"That's nice," Thea remarked. She was certain that particular bottle cost more than she'd made in a year at any of the part-time jobs she'd been allowed to have.

"Let's try another," Rita suggested. "Although we can't try too many more or you won't know which smell is which." The woman laughed and returned with another bottle. Thea smiled as Rita spritzed her again. This time the smell shocked her senses. In a whoosh it brought back the memories of the night her father had been killed and the dream she'd had. The smell reminded her of something or someone. The memory lingered like the scent of vanilla against her skin.

Ronin would know what to do. She glanced around the room to see if he was watching from his usual post. Another guard was there in his place.

Thea stared at herself in the mirror. She was

surrounded by people who were there solely to care for her and see to her every need. But she'd never felt more alone.

There was a light rap on the door.

"Come in," she called out.

The door opened and Ronin's brother entered. If she hadn't remembered him from the other night, she'd have recognized him immediately. He had the same build as Ronin. He wore his hair shorter, but the color was the same dirty blond. It was his eyes that gave him away, however. They held the same mischievous yet troubled look. She hadn't seen him since the night at the van and she didn't remember him dressed the way he was now. Today he wore a suit and an earpiece. He looked the part of head of security.

"Your Highness," he greeted her with the bow that still took her by surprise. "I'm not sure if you remember me from our first meeting. My name is Jarrod Parrish. I'll be handling your security until it is officially transferred over to the Royal Guard."

Of course she remembered him. She doubted any of the Parrish men were easy to forget. It was his words, though, that caught her by surprise.

"I thought it was members of the Royal Guard who were trying to kill me." It hardly seemed like a good idea to turn over her safety to them anytime soon.

"They were, but now that you have been proven to be a rightful heir to the throne, it would be foolish to attempt to harm you."

"And you don't think the person who wants me dead capable of being foolish?"

He shot her the look then, the one just like Ronin had when they'd first met. The one that said he wasn't quite sure what to think or say.

"I would imagine anyone who would try to harm you would be quite foolish," he answered. "Which is why we will not be handing over the responsibility until we have no doubt you are safe."

"I'm not safe now," Thea stated. She wouldn't be safe until the person who had been pulling the strings was found. But she hoped he'd take her response as a question. She was curious what answers he had. She was tired of being left out of the loop. When he didn't offer any response, she added, "Am I?"

"You are safe as long as you don't leave your rooms. There are guards posted at every possible entrance."

Another thing this man had in common with his brother was the ability to say a lot and not really answer a question. Thea grew impatient for honest, complete answers, not the watered-down versions. Of course she was safe as long as she stayed in one spot, where she could be watched over constantly.

She felt like a caged animal. Every once in a while they'd toss her a pretty dress or shoes to keep her pacified. She was tired of being treated like a prisoner. She was supposed to be a princess, after all.

Maybe it was time she started acting like one.

"Ronin told me your father was imprisoned for killing the king," she said.

"Allegedly" was his only reply.

"Was he tried and found guilty?" Thea hadn't had a chance to do any research herself to see what the official reports said about what had happened. She only knew what Ronin had told her. She wanted to know more. She needed to know why the man who had rescued her had been treated so badly.

"He was." His face hardened. A muscle at his jaw twitched. The same reaction always showed when Ronin was troubled.

"If it is within my power to make this right, I will." She wasn't sure what sort of power she held, but surely when Leo arrived he would be able to set things right. Ronin trusted his brother and she did, too. He was a good man. She could see that just as she'd seen it in Ronin.

The very fact that he'd risen above the dishonor they'd tried to bring on his father showed that.

"My brothers and I would be honored if you would," he replied with an appreciative gleam in his eyes.

"Speaking of your brother," Thea began. It was about time for him to make an appearance. "I want to see him." Even to her own ears her voice didn't quite carry the authority she was going for. But she was sure her hands on her hips and the steady gaze she leveled at the man did.

The man gave her the same slightly surprised look Ronin would have. A muscle at his rugged jaw tensed, then relaxed. For a moment she thought he might smile. But he didn't. "As you wish, Your Highness."

She watched him as he backed out the door.

At least she finally had figured out how to get things done around here.

They wanted a princess, and they had one. She was new to being in charge, being royalty, but it was in her blood. Thea straightened her back and prayed for the strength she would need to get through the next few days. The princess they had kept hidden wasn't the same princess they'd gotten back.

She had come to Denver with one purpose in mind. There would be no more hiding out and waiting for the person behind the curtain to expose themselves. She could think of only one thing that would once and for all put an end to the pain that had plagued Ronin's family as well as hers. They would have to draw the person out.

They just needed the right bait.

"She is some woman."

Ronin snorted. Even the sound reminded him of her. It was just the sort of thing she'd do when he surprised her or said something that caught her off guard.

"She's demanded to see you." His brother relayed the message he'd just received from Thea.

"Demanded?"

"Yeah. Pretty much."

Ronin scribbled his signature across the paper he'd just finished reading. It was his statement. A piece of paper that laid out every detail of what had happened since he'd met Thea. Surprisingly, even though every bit of information was there, the words didn't begin to cover the experience of being with Thea.

She'd been on his mind. He'd been with her throughout her transformation, watching as she'd changed from an ordinary woman into a princess. He'd been on duty outside her door earlier today and caught glimpses of her as the woman they'd brought in to assist her carried dresses and shoes in and out of her room. He missed Thea. Glimpses were not enough.

But he would have to get used to it. Seeing her and not being able to reach out and take her hand was one of the most difficult things he'd ever done. Seeing her just a little bit every day killed him inside.

Not seeing her at all would be easier. But he had promised to stay with her until they were sure she was safe. And she was not safe yet.

No matter how he felt, he was going to have to get used to distance. She was the princess now. Their time together had brought him something he'd never thought he would find, but that moment in time was all it could be. He was not the sort of man a princess wanted, and he would never be settled for. Even if by some strange occurrence she could want him in her life, he could never be the sidekick to a princess.

His faith might have been something he'd neglected through the years, but it was vital to him. His basic core belief was that a man should be the head of his home. How could a man be head of royalty when he was just a normal person?

It wasn't possible.

"You've got it bad, don't you?" Jarrod remarked after intently studying him for a few moments.

"Don't know what you're talking about."

"Of course you do." His brother reached across the desk, flicking at a stack of papers. "You do not like paperwork."

"Someone has to do it."

"Someone who is hiding out," his brother remarked. He pulled out a chair across from Ronin's desk and took a seat. "It isn't like you to ask to sit at a desk."

Ronin had no argument for that. He *was* hiding out.

"I needed a job." He shrugged the admission off.

"You had a job."

"And I did it," he snapped. Ronin glanced up at his brother's face, expecting to see that he was offended by the harsh tone he'd taken. Instead he saw his smug smile. There was no use trying to deny the facts with his brother. He was too perceptive. "Will she ever be safe?"

"Is anyone ever safe?" his brother asked.

"You know what I mean."

"She is safe as long as she doesn't leave the room. But someday she's going to have to leave the room."

Thea likely hated being trapped in that

room. She was probably already pacing the floors and getting that closed-in feeling. She was restless. That was probably why she'd demanded to see him.

"Someday like tonight?" Ronin questioned. They were planning to transfer her to the royal estate just outside Denver and officially present her as Princess Dorthea. High-ranking officials were to be there along with the current king for a formal dinner party in honor of the princess.

"I don't know if we're ready for that," his brother replied.

"Will we ever be ready?" He couldn't imagine there would ever be a good time to present her. But doing so might very well be the only hope they had of finally drawing the killer out. They still had nothing substantial that would link the king or anyone under him to any of the attacks on Thea's life, let alone her father's murder. "Another good reason for me to finish this up." Ronin turned his attention back to the stacks of paper on his desk. The evidence they needed was here somewhere, it had to be. He refused to believe they'd come this far to send her into the lion's den with no solid idea which lion meant to devour her.

"If you don't go see her, she's going to come find you."

Ronin stopped what he was doing and looked up at his brother. He knew Thea well enough to know Jarrod was right. He had tried to walk a fine line and keep his promise with a little distance as well, but if she wanted to see him, she would not give up.

He couldn't keep watching her from a distance and never explain things to her. Leaving things unfinished between them was a coward's way out.

His brother was right. He'd put off seeing her because he wasn't sure he could handle what he might see in her eyes. But she deserved to hear it from him. She also deserved to know what information they'd gleaned so far from the men who had attacked her the night she arrived in Denver. They might not have solid leads to who the person behind the attacks was, but it was only a matter of time. They had phone records and the men to continue questioning.

Ronin made his way through the large home his brother had turned into a safe haven for Thea. As he turned into the hallway that would take him to Thea's private suites, he pulled his cell phone from his pocket and started jabbing numbers. He had a promise to keep.

Outside the door he waited until he was sure the call was connected, then he rapped lightly.

"Come in." His heart lurched at the warmth in her voice. It drew him to her even through the heavy wood door. He steeled himself for what was sure to be an assault to the walls he had determined to keep between them and pushed the door open.

There was nothing he could have done to prepare himself for the sight of her. A green gown of beading and layers of wispy, gossamer tulle flowed over her body. The sight of her took his breath away. Her eyes met his in the mirror like a punch to the gut.

He'd always found her beautiful. Even in baggy sweats he'd thought her the loveliest woman he'd ever seen. Dressed from head to toe like the princess she was, she was stunning. His mind raced, trying to find just the right words to express half of the thoughts tumbling through his head.

"You clean up nice." That was all he could manage. Rational thought, for the time being, seemed to have vacated his brain.

"This old thing?" She laughed, twirling around so he could get the full effect of the gauzy gown. Her laughter warmed his heart and he clenched his fists to keep from moving toward her. It was then that he remembered the phone in his hand.

"I have a promise to you that I need to keep."

He held the phone to his ear. "Are you still there?" he asked into it.

After hearing the reply at the other end of the line, he handed the phone over to her. Her fingers brushed his as she took it. The simple touch was nearly his undoing. Her eyes looked up into his, full of questioning.

"It's for you," he said.

"Hello?" She spoke cautiously into the phone. He waited for the realization to come. It didn't take long. Her eyes widened and then pooled with tears. They would be tears of joy this time. "Leo!" she squealed.

She bounced up and down in place, the expression of joy on her face filling him with happiness. It warmed his heart to have been a part of their reunion, even if it were only by phone for now. He smiled. He backed from the room slowly, unable to take his eyes off her. She chattered into the phone, firing questions away at top speed. There was no way her brother could get a word in edgewise, he was sure.

When he reached the door he allowed himself one last glance. He'd meant to talk to her and explain things, but more than anything else he knew she needed this time with her brother. He would give her privacy to chat with him.

He'd known it would make her happy to know that Leo had been discharged from the hospital and was safe. Soon they would be reunited. For now it was enough that she was happy. He would know that he had some small part in that happiness. He closed the door behind him with a click. It would be impossible to forget the time he'd shared with her.

He wasn't sure he even wanted to.

THIRTEEN

The smile died on her face.

Moments before Thea had been so happy to hear her brother's voice she'd been floating on a cloud, barely paying any attention to her surroundings. She knew better. Staying aware of the things and people around her was something she'd done for so long, it was almost second nature.

Despite what they'd told her, what they'd promised, even here she was not safe.

The piece of paper propped against the pillow on her bed was proof of that.

Tonight you die.

The hastily scrawled words chilled her to the bone.

And where was Ronin? She'd been so happy when he'd handed over the phone, and she hadn't expected him to sneak away and leave her alone. Especially not when she was obviously still in danger. Thea grabbed the note from her bed and bolted from the room.

The guard they'd placed at her door yelled for her to stop, but she paid him no attention. She was a princess and she would go where she pleased. She stopped dead in her tracks as she turned a corner and the realization hit her. She had no idea where she was going.

"Where is Ronin Parrish?" she shouted to the guard behind her. He couldn't have gotten far in the short time she'd spent on the phone with Leo.

"Your Highness, you aren't supposed to leave your room," the young guard replied. "It's not safe."

"Where is Ronin Parrish?" she asked again. She smoothed down her dress and straightened her back, but even then she wasn't at his eye level. Only then did she realize she was barefoot. She stood on tiptoe and shot him her most regal look. "If you don't take me to him, I will wander every hall in this home until I find him. How safe would that be?"

For a few moments she wasn't sure if he was going to acknowledge her words. Then he sighed and motioned for her to go to the left. She took off down the hall, the guard close behind her shouting directions at her as she stormed through rooms and more hallways.

"Is this how you protect me?" Thea shouted from the doorway when she'd finally reached her destination and saw Ronin seated behind a desk.

She moved closer to the desk where Ronin sat, pen in hand, and glared down at him. Gone were the jeans and T-shirt he'd worn the short time they'd been together. Now he wore a suit and tie. The combination of clothing accentuated his muscles, making him look very strong and masculine. But it wasn't the clothing that gave him the dangerous quality. It was the look in his eyes.

"Princess, you should not have left your room."

"So I've been told," she said, motioning to the entourage of private security at her heels. "But leaving my room seems to be the only way I can have a conversation with you."

Ronin rose from his desk. Leaning across it, he stared straight into her eyes. She was sure he meant to use some form of intimidation technique. She was just as sure it wouldn't work. She leaned toward him, meeting his gaze.

"Here I am, Princess," he spoke, his voice

filled with what sounded like annoyance. "What did you need to talk to me about?"

"My safety." Thea paused and looked around. Every eye in the room was on her. She didn't let that stop her from saying what she'd come here to say. "I *thought* I was being protected here."

"You are well protected if you remain in your rooms."

"Does this look well protected to you?" Thea tossed the note she clutched in her hand at him. It bounced against his chest and rolled onto the desk. She waited for his reaction. Surprise lit his face as he reached for the crumpled paper.

She crossed her arms in front of her and waited. She wanted answers from him, and she wasn't moving until she got them.

"Where did you get this?" he asked, his brow furrowed with concern.

"It was on my bed," she replied. "Propped against my pillow."

"When?" While he waited for her to answer his question, he picked up the phone and started pushing numbers. "When?" he repeated.

"I came straight here as soon as I found it."

"Go to lockdown," he shouted into the phone at her answer. "No one comes in or out without talking with me first. And get Jarrod!"

Satisfied that she'd gotten his attention, Thea sat in the chair across from him, her dress billowing out in puffs around her. "I suppose you are going to tell me to go to my room now?"

"No!" Ronin said loudly. "You need to stay right where you are," he said more gently as he took his seat behind the desk.

"Why did you leave me after bringing me the phone?" She already knew the answer. He had hoped the phone call to her brother would distract her. It had worked. She had waited such a long time to talk to Leo. She wasn't going to just hang up on him when she'd noticed Ronin sneaking away.

She would be forever grateful that Ronin had thought to give her that time with her brother. When they would finally be together was one of the many things that had been on her mind the past few days. But just as often she'd wondered about Ronin and what had happened to cause a change in his behavior toward her. He'd been ignoring her, and none too subtly.

"I felt you needed privacy for your call and I had other things that needed my attention."

His words stung. Was she just a thing to him now? She'd come to him with so much on her mind. She needed to thank him. She needed to be sure he was okay. She needed to tell him about the perfume and the note. But none of that seemed important as she looked into his eyes.

There was something final there.

"So that's the way it is now? Now that we are here and I have to play the part of the princess, we're no longer friends? Am I just a thing for you to protect?"

"This is no part you are playing, and you are not a thing. You are Princess Dorthea and I am your servant."

The words hit Thea like a punch to the gut. Her breath whooshed out in disbelief. "You are not my servant. You are my friend." That he thought so little of what they'd shared stung.

"I was very truthful with you all along, Princess. Bringing you home safely was always what this was about. Now that I have done that, my job is finished."

Thea shook with a volatile mixture of pain and rage. He felt more—she knew he did.

Fear and doubt reared their ugly heads. She pushed them aside.

For a moment she saw a hint of the old Ronin. His face softened but only momentarily.

"Safely? You think your job is finished and I'm safe?" Thea pointed to the note in front of him. "I think that proves otherwise."

Ronin smoothed the note she'd tossed at

him out on his desk. He stared down at it, his face stony and cold. Thea knew he'd had time to read it multiple times by now. It was only three words. Three hateful, evil words. Thea squirmed in her chair, and he looked up at her.

An awkward silence filled the room.

"The men who grabbed me that night…" Thea cleared her throat and scooted forward in her seat. "Are they both locked up?"

"Yes, they are. We have been questioning them, but so far they haven't given us any useful information. They both had cell phones on them and we've been going through all the phone records and bringing in anyone they had contact with over the past few months."

"Then someone else who wants me dead is still out there," Thea whispered. There would always be someone else out there until the person behind it all was exposed. They would keep sending people until there was no one left to send. Or until she was dead.

"There is still one number we haven't been able to track down. It was obviously a burner phone."

"So it's a dead end." But she refused to believe it was that hopeless. She struggled to remain calm and not show the myriad of emotions coursing through her. She could still think of only one way that they could end this all, but she knew Ronin wouldn't like it.

Thea thought of voicing her ideas, but she knew he wouldn't listen. He was closing himself off from her and she had no idea how to make him stop. She wanted her friend back. She wanted the man who had laughed with her and treated her like a normal person. The only problem was, short of begging, she had no idea how to topple the walls he'd erected around himself.

"I have things to do to get ready for meeting the king tonight," Thea said as she rose from the chair.

"I won't allow it," Ronin stated as he rose across from her. "It's too dangerous."

"Allow?" Thea hated to pull rank on him and she knew it would only put more distance between them if she did, but this was her life. She was tired of running in circles waiting for the next threat to expose itself. "Dangerous or not, it could be the only way we'll ever prove who is trying to kill me." Fear clutched at her heart, squeezing it. Her throat tightened with the weight of her decision. "I'm going, with or without you and your protection."

Thea waited for the argument that she knew would come, but Ronin stood speechless by his desk. His eyes bore into hers. He knew she was right. He just couldn't bring himself to face the facts she already had. It was the only way. "I'm going back to my room. If you don't think I'll be safe there, you're welcome to come stand guard at my door."

And with that she turned, lifted the hem of her gown just above her calves and stormed from the room. She could hear Ronin behind her. After the note, he would double-and-triple-check before letting anyone else near her. She was sure of that.

Mixed emotions rolled through her. The fear was still there, but it was buried deep beneath the despair of rejection. She knew how deep and true the feelings she had for Ronin were. She had hoped the time they'd had together, no matter how short, had also shown him what they shared was real.

His silence behind her said otherwise.

She prayed as she ran back to her room. She needed time alone to clear her head and listen for that still, small voice that would lead her in the right direction. If she would even be alone in her room and there wasn't someone waiting and lurking in the shadows to kill her. Being bait for a murderer might not be the smartest move, but it was the only way she could see to ever end this.

Thea threw open the door to her rooms and

waited quietly as Ronin did a thorough check. After a few moments he left without a word and she ran to her bed. Lying across it, she let the flood of emotions go and sobbed. He cared for her. She sensed it. He was just afraid. Fear was something she was used to, as well. He was a strong man, but she wasn't sure he was strong enough to let go of whatever was holding him back and keeping him from admitting his true feelings for her.

Ronin read the crumpled note again. The words filled with hatred jumped out at him. Bold black strokes against the white sheet of paper. "Tonight you die," it read. Anger bubbled up inside him. He was sure it wasn't the guards he'd posted. He'd only posted men at her door that he'd worked with and knew personally. Still, someone had gotten that close. They had been in her room. Why hadn't they just killed her then?

He slammed his fist down on the desk. All movement in the room stopped as every eye turned toward him.

"Get me Jarrod!" he yelled. His gaze moved over the crumpled paper. It would be unlikely they'd find any usable prints on it. But it was worth a try. If he could get the prints lifted from it here, it would be quicker. But they'd probably have to leave that to Jarrod's contacts with the police.

That would be more time lost.

He shook the thought from his mind. Whatever the reasons, he was thankful they hadn't harmed her. He had thought she would be safe here. There were guards everywhere. He'd known the deception ran deep, but perhaps it was deeper than they had even begun to realize.

The troubled look in her eyes as she'd thrown the note at him flashed through his mind. He hadn't wanted to hurt her. Treating her that way and putting the distance between them were the hardest things he'd ever done. But the words were the truth as he saw it and he needed the distance to keep himself from reaching for her.

They couldn't have any sort of future. She was a princess. She would marry a dignitary if not a prince from a neighboring nation. She would marry into wealth and her children would be heirs to the throne after her.

The only place a man like him had in her life was to protect her, and he wasn't even doing a good job of that. He'd let his emotions get in the way. That was just the thing he'd been most afraid of. All of the distancing and assigning new bodyguards to her hadn't helped at all. She was still in his mind and she was still in danger.

"You needed me?" Jarrod asked.

"Yes." Ronin battled to rid all emotion from his voice and relay the facts to his brother. He would need every bit of information he could give him to help find the person behind these threats. "There's been another threat against Princess Dorthea's life." Ronin picked up the note and handed it over. "Have we been able to trace the last number from the phones?"

"No. It was evidently a burner phone. It's either been disposed of or never turned back on."

"We have to assume they are smart enough to have gotten rid of it by now."

"I agree." His brother's expression clouded as he skimmed the note before handing it back over. "When did this happen?"

"She brought it in about thirty minutes ago." Fear knotted in his stomach. "Meanwhile we have someone in the building with access to the princess who we cannot trust. Are you completely sure about the men you have put on her detail?"

"They have all been with me for years. I've known some of them since they were kids. No one has gotten into that room without being thoroughly checked."

"Well, someone got in." Ronin took a deep

breath to keep from shouting. It wouldn't do anyone any good if he let his frustration run rampant on everyone. His brother didn't deserve this. He'd worked just as hard over the years to finally get to the truth. "I've locked the building down. Whoever did this should still be here."

"I'll start a sweep. Everyone who has been near her room will be questioned first," Jarrod said even as he called a man over to begin the process.

"She wants to continue with the event tonight." Ronin shook his head as he spoke the words. She would be in grave danger. But it was a good plan.

If it were anyone else he would be all for it. But it was Thea. He didn't like it. Moving her to the Royal Estate and attending the reception that had been planned for her tonight would be suicide. There would be too many unknowns.

"She what?" his brother questioned.

It was obvious his brother shared his sentiments.

"It's a good plan." He hated to admit it, but unless they could find the person behind it all before tonight, they might have to go along with it.

"I'll have the note checked for prints," his brother said. Then he stopped at the doorway and turned back toward him. "This isn't the Dark Ages, you know. It's obvious you two care for each other. The princess is free to see anyone she chooses. It's not like it's in the rule book that she has to marry someone of equal rank or bloodline. Even if it was, she strikes me as the sort of person who would challenge it for something she wanted."

Ronin smiled. She was that very sort. She would do what she wanted if it was for the good of her or her country or anyone else. That knowledge hardened his resolve. Thea would feel as if she had to choose between him and her country, whether she actually had to or not. Ronin would not be the man to put her in that position. Not when so many had done so much to put her back in her rightful place.

"Aren't you getting that note checked?" Ronin asked, hoping to change the subject and remind his brother of his mission.

Jarrod nodded. "We have a lot to do to get ready for tonight. I'll also double up the security on the princess without making it too obvious."

"I want to be with her." If they were actually going to let her go through with attending tonight, he had to be there. Too much was at stake to entrust her safety to anyone else.

Ronin handed Jarrod the folder that contained all the information they'd gathered so far and the statements from those who had been brought in already. Thankfully, only a handful of Guardsmen had been involved. They had to have been getting their orders from someone. But so far none of them were talking.

The obvious guess was the king himself. Ronin had met the man once. It had been years ago, but he hadn't seemed the treacherous type. But he also knew it wasn't always the obvious person who was capable of doing things you'd least expect. Given the way this person had infiltrated such an honorable group of men, it would seem they must be very closely tied to the king in some way.

"Well, then I suggest you get ready for your big night. The cars should be around in about—" Jarrod paused to glance at his watch "—an hour."

"Fine, but someone needs to be on top of tracking this last number. There's still a threat out there."

"I'm on top of it. Just keep her close. This will be their last chance before it all becomes official and she returns home."

Ronin double-and triple-checked the assignments of cars and drivers before heading to his room and changing into something more appropriate for being at the side of a princess. He checked his weapon and communication, as well. When he was positive everything was ready, he made his way to Thea's room.

Once there, he paused. His hand froze in midair near the door. Everything was ready but him. A few hours ago when she'd come to his office he'd thought he'd once and for all ended the chance of anything they might have had. He was wrong. She was right. He cared for her, more than he wanted to admit, even to himself. When push came to shove she'd stepped up and made the decision he hadn't wanted to. She'd offered herself up as bait.

Tonight someone would try to kill her, and he was afraid. He wasn't a stranger to fear, but this sort of fear was new to him. Not being in control was even newer. Nobody controlled Thea. He'd learned that lesson the hard way. She was a very special sort of woman. Being with her and not being able to hold her and tell her of his true feelings would be hard. But it was what he was going to have to do. Tonight she would be put on display for the world to see. It might be just a small dinner party, but the who's who in their government's ring of influential people would be there. It would be her reappearance into the world that would now be hers.

She would be a bright and shiny lure in a room possibly containing a hungry shark circling, just watching and waiting for the chance to strike. And they were no closer in knowing for sure who that person was than they were days ago. No matter how difficult it would be to be with her for tonight, it was the smart thing to do. He would protect her with his life, just as he'd promised to do when he'd first gone looking for her.

Ronin took a deep breath and knocked.

"Come in." Her voice was barely discernible through the door. He opened it and saw why. She stood at the far side of the room, the balcony doors open to the view of the majestic Rocky Mountain range on display. The sun was just beginning to set behind their white-topped peaks.

"It's beautiful," she whispered.

He'd nearly forgotten her sleepy confession of wanting to see the mountains. He would have liked to have been with her when she saw them for the first time, but this would do. Sharing this moment with her brought a warmth to his heart.

He stepped into the room and shut the door behind him.

Even more beautiful than the view of the sunset-lit sky was the sight of her. She was dressed for the evening ahead. Her hair framed her face perfectly in a loose, twisted updo. Ringlets of russet brown drew attention to her soft features and large green eyes. She turned toward him, closing the balcony doors behind her. As she drew closer, he could see those eyes were also red and puffy.

He'd hurt her. The knowledge stabbed at his gut. She wore the tiara that had been in her family for ages. One large emerald stood in the center of the platinum framing, sprinkled with diamonds and smaller emeralds. Matching teardrop earrings hung against her long, elegant neck.

"You look breathtaking." Those words weren't enough to describe her appearance, but he had to try.

"It's the same dress I had on earlier," she stated, twirling, sending the layers of green into a rustling motion around her. "It is beautiful, but…"

"But?" he asked.

"I don't want to seem unappreciative, but I feel like a fraud. I don't feel at all like me."

"You are very much you." She was the most amazing woman he'd ever met, princess or not. "We've gone to great lengths to verify that."

"You know what I mean." She sighed. "I think I'd trade it all away to be back in the farmhouse in Kansas." The wistfulness of her voice had him wondering if she didn't truly mean it.

"You'll get used to it."

"Used to it?" she questioned. Her eyes filled with confusion. He could understand. This had to be a huge change for her. "But should I have to get used to being myself, or shouldn't I just be myself?"

"I think you will find that your people will accept you being whoever you want to be."

"But you didn't."

The simple fact floored him. He couldn't think of a valid argument for her words.

The truth of the matter was he did accept her. She was Princess Dorthea. As the princess she had his respect and his loyalty. He couldn't think of her in any other way. He should never have allowed himself to grow so close to her. Whether he liked it or not, he knew what was best for her. Given time, he was sure she'd come to the same conclusion.

There was a light rap on the door and Ronin opened it to find Jarrod standing outside.

"The car is ready," he said.

Thea grabbed her wrap and moved past him. He struggled with the desire to reach out to her, to take her in his arms and once again tell her that everything would be okay. Instead, he followed along behind her as she made her way outside to the vehicles waiting to whisk her away to her future.

"I still don't like this," he whispered as he held the car door open for her and she stepped inside.

"I know," she replied. "But it will all be over soon and then you won't have to be bothered with my safety anymore."

FOURTEEN

A hush fell over the room as she entered through the large double doors of the royal estate. Her stomach clenched in fear. Thea took a deep breath. Someone in this room of strangers wanted her dead.

Part of her wanted to turn and run. She knew how to disappear. She'd lived her life that way. She could do it again. She would do it better this time. She'd hide so well even Ronin wouldn't find her. But was that what she really wanted?

She shook the thoughts away and took another step. She could feel Ronin's strength. He wouldn't get too close, but knowing he was there helped. She could do this. If she didn't, she wouldn't be just letting her country down, but her brother and all of those who had come before her. She would not be a disappointment to her family.

She took another step. She thought of those

who had served her country loyally and been paid with death or imprisonment. Ronin's father would finally be freed and his name cleared once she was granted the authority to do so. When the real killer stepped out of the shadows and showed their true nature, they could all start their new lives.

She glanced behind her to be sure Ronin was nearby. She wished he'd move to her side, take her hand and help her face this new life that scared her so much. He nodded but stayed just behind her, despite her willing him closer.

Every eye in the room was on her. She felt as if she was on display. In a way she was. Everyone was here to see this princess who had been in hiding all these years. She'd known her father had been loved and respected, and she would be accepted just because of that. But she hoped her people would learn to love her, as well. Not for her father, but for who she was on her own.

Thea took another deep breath and prayed for the strength to keep moving.

Her eyes swept over the room, hoping to recognize at least one person among the guests. She wished Leo were here. The knowledge that he would be soon gave her strength.

The threat hid somewhere in this room of strangers. Once it was eliminated she could have her brother back. She could have her life back, any life she wanted.

That should have put her mind at ease at least a little. But it didn't. For that to happen, she had to get through tonight. She had to lure the person behind it all, the person who wanted her dead, out into the open.

Thea took another deep breath. Head held high, she made her way to the other side of the room.

Guest after guest was brought to her and introduced. Some of the names she recognized as people her father had known, but she'd just been a child and hadn't yet been introduced formally to most of them.

None of them seemed like the sort of person who would want her dead. They seemed friendly and excited and genuinely happy to have her return. But still she felt it, the shiver of fear lurking just behind her smile. As pleased as she was to meet those who seemed happy to see her alive, with every handshake and nod she wondered if this was the person who wanted her dead.

The thought lingered, but she kept reminding herself that she would not be the victim tonight. Ronin was close by and she knew he'd rush to her side if any slight threat were to show itself. It was his job. She was his job. He'd made that point painfully clear.

She could feel him watching her. His strength gave her the needed boost to continue through the evening. Part of her wanted the night to go on and on and never end. When it ended, his job might be over. If the threat were discovered, he would think she no longer needed his protection. But she would always need him.

Although she didn't treasure the thought of living in danger for the rest of her life, she didn't like the idea of going on without him, either.

Her eyes swept the room, taking in the grandeur of it all. A large crystal chandelier hung in the center of the room. Fine paintings adorned the walls. The extravagance was shocking. Days ago she'd been happy to come up with enough spare change to get a bag of potato chips from a snack machine. Tonight, uniformed waiters and waitresses carried silver trays filled with the most delicious-looking appetizers she'd ever seen.

As much as she was in amazement of it all, she knew this was not her life. It would have been if she'd never been ripped from it. But she had been. She had lived another life; she'd been another person. Some might not understand it.

She knew many would see what had happened to her as tragic. They would take pity on her circumstances, but she didn't want their pity. God had taken something awful and turned it into something beautiful. She smiled at the thought. So many times she'd questioned why things had happened the way they had. But now, in this moment, she realized that without the pain of the past, she wouldn't have learned to love who she really was deep inside.

Life had been rough, but through that she had learned to love and appreciate the small things. The things many people took for granted. A waiter passed by with a tray of appetizers. He held the tray out for her and she perused the delicacies. She didn't know what half of the stuff was, which made her wary, but she was hungry and surely the food would have been prepared with her allergies in mind.

In her peripheral vision she could see Ronin's steady gaze on her.

In his eyes she could see all those things he wouldn't admit to feeling. It gave her hope. He nodded in acknowledgment and she took a bite.

He might think he was only doing his duty and didn't really care for her, but she knew he did. She felt it. She only had to find a way to show him, and if she had to be in danger to do it, then so be it.

Thea continued mingling with the guests. The hope that burned in her heart that Ronin would admit his real feelings put a new spin on the evening. She would enjoy the night. Ronin might be unwilling to accept that he cared for her, but she would cherish being with him, even if he was keeping himself at a distance.

Thea could tell when the mood of the room changed. The murmurs rolled like a wave through the guests, and then the small group beside her parted. A regally dressed man and woman stood in the opening. His tuxedo was adorned with medals and a tasseled purple sash. The woman held tight to his arm, her gown sparkling and shimmering over her slim body. The man smiled openly and stepped toward Thea. Taking her hand, he bent to place a light kiss against it.

"Princess Dorthea," he addressed her formally. "I am King Marcus Alexander Wendell. But not for much longer, I take it. It is a pleasure to see you alive after all these years."

Any thoughts of this man being behind the threats on her life fled. She could tell his joy at seeing her was genuine. There was nothing fake about the man. Thea smiled and returned his greeting.

"It is my pleasure to meet you, sir," she said. "We are family, yet I barely remember you."

"I'm not surprised. We only met a few times and we were both much younger then." The portly man patted her hand and winked. "I hope you will do me the honor of sitting at my side during the meal."

"Of course," Thea replied. "I have so much to catch up on."

"That you do." Their conversation was interrupted by the woman clearing her throat. Thea could tell immediately she didn't like being ignored. She was used to being the center of attention. She stood in place, watching Thea through lowered eyes. "Where are my manners?" the man said. "This is my lovely fiancée, Lucia Delmont."

"Your Highness," the woman greeted her. Thea knew she hadn't met her yet tonight, but there was something strangely familiar about her. The woman's gaze slid over her slowly. Thea resisted the urge to smooth her dress and check her hair. "It's an honor to meet you." The sound of the woman's voice set off warning bells in Thea's mind.

Lucia leaned in to kiss her cheek. The scent of her perfume assailed Thea. Every memory floating around the edges of her mind came forward. The smell, the voice… This was the woman in the room the night her father had

died. This was the woman who had left her for
dead, no doubt back to finish the job.

"If you will excuse me," the king said, dis-
missing himself. "There is much to arrange
and many people I must talk to before dinner.
I'll leave you ladies to get acquainted." Taking her hand again, he added, "I'll be sure to
save you that spot."

Before her mind could process a coherent
reply, she was alone with the woman. Thea
glanced around for Ronin, but he wasn't in
sight. In the spot where he had been standing
was the younger bodyguard they'd assigned to
her earlier. Her heart sank.

"Is everything all right?" Lucia asked, her
red lips thinning to a tight smile. "Would you
like a glass of water? You look a little flushed."

"Yes, thank you." If the woman left to get
something to drink, she could find Ronin. "A
glass of water would be very nice."

But the woman didn't leave.

"It's a good thing I've brought you a glass,
then." Lucia handed a glass of ice water over.
Thea took a sip, but it did nothing to steady her
nerves. She tried to smile, remain calm and not
let on that she had recognized her voice. After
all these years the voice had a face.

"It is nice to see you have made it home,
safe and sound." The words said one thing, but

the woman's demeanor said something totally opposite. "I guess you are hardly home now really, though, but you have made it this far."

"Yes." Her skin heated. "I have." Any other words stuck in her throat. A tingling sensation began in her fingers, working its way up her arm. Her throat tightened. She needed Ronin. She needed to tell him now what she'd remembered.

"Is something wrong?" the woman questioned.

"No," Thea replied. "Everything is fine." Thea choked the words out through her tightening throat. But it wasn't. Something was wrong. Her thoughts muddled in her mind and her hands began to tremble. She tried to make eye contact with the young man currently acting as her guard. Short of screaming out for him, she could only hope he'd notice her discomfort.

"If you'll excuse me…" Thea attempted to walk away. She had to find Ronin.

Lucia's eyebrows arched in question. "Are you looking for a guard?" Her voice remained low and steady. "Look around, they are all around you, but none will help. They don't see me as a danger." The woman's hand rested against Thea's elbow in an attempt to guide her across the room. "But you do, don't you? Do you remember me?"

Thea wasn't sure how to respond. The truth hardly seemed smart when she was sure now the woman meant her harm. Every memory of that night flooded her clouded mind. Thea remembered her, or her voice at least. The voice was straight from her nightmares. It was a voice she'd never forget.

"I don't feel well," Thea replied. The faces around her blurred as she struggled to find a familiar one that might notice she was in danger. Before Thea realized what was happening, the woman had begun leading her toward the patio doors at the rear of the house. "I'm sure you don't, Princess. But don't worry. It will all be over soon."

The voice sent shivers up her spine. Thea suddenly felt hot, desperate for a breath of fresh air. It was stuffy and she felt as if the whole room were closing in around her.

"Princess, are you okay?" the young guard she had been searching for asked, suddenly appearing at her side.

"I need air," she managed to squeeze from her tightening throat. Her lips felt swollen and puffy.

"The princess is not feeling well," Lucia

stated. "Does she have any allergies? I think she's eaten something she shouldn't have."

Thea could only manage a nod as she struggled for a breath. Something was definitely wrong. She'd only had an allergic reaction once before in her life, when she was young. After that, everyone had always been so careful to be sure she was never given any form of nuts. But this felt a lot like she remembered feeling then. Her thoughts jumbled in her head.

"If you'll stay with her, I'll be right back with help."

"Of course." The woman brushed her fingers over Thea's forehead. Her hand felt cold and clammy against Thea's hot skin. The feeling only fueled her growing panic. "I'll stay with the princess."

"No," Thea croaked out on a whisper as the man's back disappeared through the guests.

The door opened and Thea sucked in a breath of much-needed fresh air as she was led outside. It burned her throat and lungs.

"Maybe you could use another sip of that water?"

Thea had nearly forgotten the glass she held in her hand and the woman at her side. She took another sip of the cool liquid. It soothed her throat and for a brief second she could breathe with ease again.

Thea's grip loosened on the glass and it fell, shattering into thousands of tiny pieces on the pebbled patio. A wave of dizziness hit her and she stumbled against the only thing she could hold on to. Grabbing at the woman's arm, she looked up into the eyes of the person she was sure meant to kill her.

"Explain this!" Ronin shouted. He slammed his hands onto the tabletop and slid the crinkled note across its smooth surface. With precise movements he pressed it out flat directly in front of the sobbing woman.

His gut twisted. She'd been crying before he'd entered the room, so he could hardly say he was the cause of her distress. But he wasn't going to take it easy on her because of it. Real or fake, tears were not going to stop him from getting to the bottom of this.

Thea's life hung in the balance.

"Why would you want to kill the princess?" Ronin glared down at the teary-eyed woman.

She was one of the few people who had access to Thea's room. She'd caved immediately and had been brought to the estate for immediate questioning. She held the answers to who wanted Thea dead. But something still didn't make sense. This woman had worked for Thea's family. She had been loyal to King

Donovan even after his death. She'd been chosen weeks ago to be brought over from the family residence in Portase to once again be a personal maid for the princess.

"I don't. I would never," she gasped. "She is a lovely girl. I don't mean her any harm at all." The words came out as strangled sounds in between heavy sobs.

"If you do not want harm to come to the princess, you will help us. We're trying to save her." Ronin stepped back from the table to keep from once again slamming his fists down on it. He didn't want to scare the woman any more than he already had.

"But you admitted to leaving the note on her bed." He pushed on.

"Yes," she sobbed. "I left the note."

"Why?" Ronin was quickly losing the little patience he had. This woman obviously wasn't the mastermind behind the attempts on Thea's life, but she had to have had contact with the person who was. She had gotten the note from someone along with the orders of what to do with it. She was their best chance at finally following the trail all the way to the person at the top.

"Why did you leave the note?" he repeated.

"I was told to leave the note. That's all I know."

"By who?" Ronin leaned closer. She was close to giving the name, he could feel it.

"If I tell you, they'll kill my son." She barely managed to get the words out before breaking out into another round of tears.

Ronin stepped back, glancing over at his brother.

"This is all we have," Jarrod said softly as he handed over a file. "She has one son. He's a cadet, first year in the Royal Academy."

They were losing time. Ronin's mind raced with how he could sway the woman to share what she knew with them. He moved back over to the table.

"Do you know who we are?" Ronin asked, motioning toward his brother and himself.

"Yes," she sobbed. "Your father was a good man."

"Do you believe we can give your son protection?" Jarrod asked.

The woman glanced at Jarrod, then back at Ronin. A glimmer of hope shimmered in her teary eyes. She nodded.

"Your son will be under our protection the second you tell us the truth about what is going on." Jarrod moved close to the table, as well. "He will be safe."

"Tell us who had you leave the note," Ronin pressed again.

Despite the hope on her face, she hesitated. "Whoever you are protecting has threatened your family. Is that really the sort of person you want to have on your side?" Ronin reached in and grabbed her hands gently. Drawing them close, he looked directly into her eyes. He hoped she'd read the sincerity there and do what was best not only for her family, but also for Thea and the country she represented.

Silence filled the room. Ronin's heart raced. He let go of her hands and backed away. Short of torture, he had done all he could do to get the name from her. She had to see that it was for the best. Once he knew the name, he'd be able to finally put an end to this nightmare Thea had lived through. She'd be able to reclaim her legacy and live her life and maybe he'd find a way to go on without her.

Ronin fisted his hands at his side to keep from reaching out and grabbing the woman. He knew she was thinking. In her mind there was a lot to weigh. But he needed the answer. The woman sat up in her chair and folded her hands on the table. Time ticked away slowly, but her eyes showed she had made her decision. He knew it would only be a matter of seconds before she finally said the words.

"Lucia Delmont."

He heard the gasp from Jarrod simultaneous to his own.

"Are you sure?" His mind raced faster than he could form the words, faster than he knew he'd be able to act.

"She is an evil woman." The woman nodded. "When she couldn't have King Donovan, she made another king she *could* have."

Her words made little sense, but he didn't have time to listen to more of her story. All the pieces from the past few days fell into place.

"I need to know where Lucia is," he said to his brother and the other guard who were already following them from the room. "Now," he added on his way down the narrow hallway. Jarrod was close on his heels. Ronin had left Thea with a young guard. He'd been a fool to let her out of his sight. He'd promised he'd protect her, and just when she needed him most he'd abandoned her.

Turning the corner he ran straight into the young man he'd left to watch Thea.

"Sir," the young man addressed him. "It's the princess. There's something wrong. She's having an allergic reaction and needs her adrenaline auto-injector."

"And you left her?" Ronin shouted.

"Lucia Delmont is with her."

It took every ounce of control he had to not

give in to the anger and tell the kid what a stupid mistake he had made for leaving her...but he'd left her, too.

Fear clutched at his heart. He'd been afraid for her life before, but this time was different. For the first time he could see what his life would be like without her in it. He didn't like what he saw. That fear must have shown on his face.

"I'll get it." His brother knew, just as he knew. The princess was in grave danger. "Go! Find Thea."

Ronin rushed into the main room, where he'd left her. He moved quickly through the crowd, searching for a glimpse of her. He couldn't lose her now, not when he'd just realized what life without her would be like.

She might hate him for the things he'd said and the way he'd acted. But if he had to be her personal servant for the rest of his life, he would take whatever seconds of her time she could spare him. He'd treasure each moment and every glance. He had been a fool for thinking he would be in her shadow.

Thea was not the sort of woman who would settle for that. She loved completely and would make her man the king of her heart no matter what his social status might be. She'd tried to share that with him, and he'd closed his heart to it.

He raced through the guests, checking every room for signs of Thea or Lucia. He couldn't be too late. He pushed the thoughts away. He wouldn't be too late. He would find her, and when he did he would tell her all the things he should have shared before. He would tell her he loved her.

FIFTEEN

He would come for her.

Thea reminded herself over and over. With each tremor of pain that shot through her body, she continued her mantra. He would rescue her. She couldn't give up hope. The night air was a relief against her burning skin but only temporarily. It was just a matter of time. She knew that. She had obviously eaten something. Or Lucia had slipped her something. Either way, she needed her auto-injector. If she didn't get it soon, she would slip more and more into a state of anaphylactic shock.

There was little doubt in her mind. If that didn't kill her, the woman would.

The cool air felt good on her skin. But the burning continued. The world spun. Her mouth dried. "If you are looking for your prince, he is not coming."

"He…" Thea tried to speak, but the words wouldn't come. Her tongue was too swollen.

She knew she needed to save her breath, to try not to let the panic overtake her.

He was that piece of her that she hadn't known was missing until she was without him and felt what being alone was truly like.

"Poor princess. It really is a shame that your homecoming will be so short-lived. But if it makes you feel any better, you will soon be reunited with your dear father." The woman moved closer and Thea took a wobbly step back.

It was then Thea became semi-aware of her surroundings. She had known they had moved farther away from the house—but not this far. In her confusion she'd let the woman maneuver her down the path that led to the dock and boathouse.

She stood out on a dock. Thin rails bordered the sides.

"At first I had thought to bring you out here and drown you. I've heard it's quite a peaceful way to go." She laughed, a vile sound that bore no empathy or compassion. "Supposedly it only hurts if you try to hold your breath." The woman glared at her. Hatred filled her eyes. "But now that I can see my peanut oil had such a lovely effect on you, I think I'll be just as happy to watch you slowly suffocate and die. It's surprising what only a few drops can do. I'm surprised you didn't taste it."

Thea choked on the breath she tried to suck in.

"Or maybe you did," Lucia continued. "Maybe you were just too busy trying to pretend you didn't recognize me. But you did, didn't you?"

Thea nodded.

"At least you are smart enough to realize there is no need for lies now." The woman's voice was a shrill sound to Thea's ears. Just like the voice in her dream.

"Why?" Thea was barely able to squeeze the word out of her tightened throat. She had to know. Why would anyone hate her so much that they'd want to watch her suffer?

The woman moved toward her and Thea stumbled back, grabbing at the rails of the dock. Her world spun in a dizzying swirl of flashes.

"I would have thought in all this time away, you would have remembered more about what happened the night your father died. That is the main reason I wanted you dead, after all. Once I found out you were still alive, I couldn't have a loose end about."

"But my father…" Thea had no strength to finish the sentence.

"The poor man. He should have married me."

The woman moved toward her again, but Thea was too weak to move away. Lucia's cold fingers brushed against her cheek. Thea turned her head from the touch.

"You are such a pretty girl. If you weren't so much older than my dear son, you would have made a lovely bride for him. It was my plan all along, you see. I would have had control of the throne one way or another. He needs a younger bride, though, and a woman who has been raised to know her place. That could never have been you, could it, Princess?"

Thea grabbed at the dock railing, struggling to pull herself up to face the woman but collapsed instead at her feet.

"You always were quite the fighter. Your father would have been so proud. But Adriana, she will make the perfect bride. When the news of her making it out of the fire is discovered, then all will be well."

"Adriana?" Thea whispered, a low croaking sound.

Darkness threatened. It kept tugging her in, pulling at her. Thea fought against it and fought to make sense of the words the woman spoke, but she was sure she couldn't be hearing her right.

"Yes, Adriana. I saved her from the fire

myself. She was such a tiny little thing. Even I have a heart, you see. I might not have to marry the sad little man at all. Not when I have a son who could be king. That is all I've ever wanted, you know. Power is everything. It would have been better for me to be queen. I would have made a good queen. But I can settle for control. When it became obvious I couldn't win your father's affections, I killed him. I thought I'd killed you and your silly brother, as well. After that it was easy to make my own king. I should have known better."

Thea's throat tightened.

In the distance she could hear the sounds of the guests still mingling. It struck her as odd that the laughter of strangers might be the last sound she heard. Then she heard it. Someone called her name.

Ronin! She wanted to shout his name. She screamed it in her mind, but she didn't have the strength left to make a sound.

"You really are hard to kill, aren't you? I can almost understand now why the men I sent to kill you failed so miserably. But if you want a job done right…" The woman paused and pushed at her, shoving her closer to the edge of the dock. "You need to do it yourself. Even the man I brought with me to kill your father couldn't do it. In the end I had to do that my-self, too."

Thea struggled to fight back. But she had no strength left in her. The little air she could breathe wheezed through her tightened throat. The voices grew closer. If she could just hang on.

"You really need to just give up and die." The woman pushed at her harder, shoving her against the edge of the dock.

Thea forced her eyes open. The woman kicked at her again, pushing against her. Thea's body toppled, falling over the edge into the freezing water below.

The water closed over her. Darkness pulled her in as she sank. She tried to swim, to fight against the weight, to suck in air, but her throat was swollen and tight. Her lungs burned.

She had to fight. She couldn't die now. She reached out, grabbing at anything. She had to hold on.

"Hold on, Thea!" Ronin shouted as he grabbed her hands tightly. He pulled hard, yanking her up over the dock edge while Lucia stood and watched, her lips turning ever so slowly into an aloof smile.

He paid the woman no attention. Jarrod wouldn't be far behind him and he'd see to her; right now he needed to get Thea out of the water.

He held Thea by the wrist, pulling her limp body up over the edge of the dock.

"You stupid, stupid man," Lucia crooned from behind him. "You have no clue what you are doing. You are ruining it all." She lunged and too late Ronin noticed the flash of steel in her hand and her intent.

Her hand rose in the air and came down quickly. Ronin moved to protect Thea, his body shielding her. The blade sliced through his coat, cutting into his shoulder.

He reacted with a wide swing of his arm, pain slicing through his body as his forearm connected with the woman, sending her sprawling. The knife fell from her hand and over the edge of the dock into the dark water.

"She needs her injection!" he yelled, hoping someone would be close enough to hear him. Where was Jarrod? He removed his coat and wrapped it around Thea. Bending over close he listened to see if she was breathing. Her lips were purple and swollen.

"Just let her die!" the woman screamed as she lunged again.

This time Ronin was ready. He pulled his gun and aimed it directly at her face.

"Not another word!" Ronin pulled Thea

close and glared up at the woman. Lucia took a step away. "Don't you dare move. Not an inch. If you move again I will shoot you." It wasn't an empty threat. She had tried to kill Thea. Part of him hoped she would push him and see what happened.

He'd arrived at the dock just in time to see Lucia kick Thea over the edge. In that moment he could have killed her. Surprisingly, she hadn't been his first thought. Thea had been.

He kept his gun aimed at Lucia, but even now he was more worried for Thea than what might happen to the other woman. For all he cared she could run. They knew who she was now. They knew her plan and just how evil she could be. There was no place she could hide that she wouldn't be found.

For now, Thea was his concern. He held her close to his body for warmth. Her breathing was shallow, but she was alive.

His heart raced through the possible outcomes. She was in shock. She could die. Time ticked by slowly; it felt like hours, but within minutes Jarrod was there. Ronin reached out for the auto-injector that would give her the boost of adrenaline she needed. Quickly he gave her the shot in her upper thigh.

"I've already called for an ambulance, but it could be a while."

"I'm going to take her to the house and see if we can get her warm." Ronin scooped her up in his arms. "Do you have her?" he asked, nodding toward the woman who had caused them so much pain.

"Yes." Jarrod grabbed Lucia's arm, pulling it behind her back and cuffing her.

His shoulder burned and he could feel the warmth of blood seeping through his clothing. None of it mattered.

Thea was safe. He pulled her limp body close. She couldn't die now, not when he'd finally realized how much he truly cared for her.

Ronin made his way back up to the house. Thea needed to be warmed as quickly as possible and monitored. If her breathing didn't return to normal soon, she might need another injection.

The guests still mingling in the main room spread out, leaving him room to carry her through to a lounge chair in front of the fire.

Where was the ambulance? Ronin held her limp hands in his. He felt helpless. There was nothing he could do now but wait. He watched her intently, searching for any signs that she would be okay. Her skin was so pale.

"What can I do?" Jarrod asked from behind him.

"Where is Lucia?" Ronin choked the words out.

"She is secure and the police are on their way."

"Good." Ronin nodded and began rubbing Thea's hands between his own. "Bring me blankets." He pulled the chair over closer to the fire. She needed the heat. "And double-check on that ambulance." Helplessness was not a feeling he was used to, but he'd felt it so many times the past few days. Every time they'd had a moment when they weren't sure what to do, Thea had prayed. Her faith had been so strong, it had almost seemed strong enough for the both of them. But now she was weak. She needed him now, more than she'd ever needed him before. She needed him to be strong. It was in that instant that Ronin knew. The only thing he could do for her was pray.

She needed him to have the same strong faith that she'd shown through their whole journey. She needed a man who was not only strong physically and emotionally, but who also could have that same strong faith she had. That would be the sort of man who would see her through the rest of her life, the ups and downs that they would have no control over.

The sort of man who knew when they were at the end of what they could do and needed to let go and see what God could do.

He knelt by her side, took her hand and closed his eyes. He could be that man. He let go, trusted and prayed. "Please, God. Don't take her away from me now. I need her." He paused, searching his heart for the words. "I love her."

He felt her hand move and opened his eyes. Her eyes fluttered open.

"Ronin," she whispered.

"Shh...don't talk." Ronin's fingers tightened around hers. He knew talking would be painful and she needed to give her body a chance to warm and for the swelling to go down. But she would be okay. "You're safe. You're going to be okay." He gave voice to the thoughts racing through his mind.

She would be okay. God had heard him. He knew that.

She swallowed hard, a grimace crossing her features. She was still in pain, but her breathing was returning to normal and a pink flush slowly seeped back into her skin.

Every bit of fear he'd had was chased away by a moment of complete peace. He looked into her eyes and saw all the love that had been there earlier when he'd turned her away. He'd hurt her.

He would never hurt her again.

Her hand tightened around his. She didn't have to say a word; it was in her eyes. They were filled with love. A love he didn't deserve but was so happy to have.

"I almost lost you," he said, swiping a lock of wet hair from her face.

She shook her head. "Not that easy," she whispered.

Ronin smiled, the love in his heart spreading. He knew he was grinning like a lovesick fool, but he didn't care. She really was going to be okay if she had her wits about her enough to tease him.

"The ambulance just passed the gate." His brother laid his hand on his shoulder. It was then Ronin remembered the room full of people surrounding them.

"No hospital," she croaked out.

"Yes, hospital," Ronin corrected. "You need to be checked out to be sure everything is okay."

"I'm fine," she argued while struggling in her wet gown to sit upright.

"This is the way it's going to be, Princess," Ronin said, leaning over close so his words wouldn't be heard by everyone. "I'm not taking no for an answer."

He knew she'd have more to say about that if she could talk without pain, but he was spared anything she might have said by the EMTs wheeling a gurney through.

He stepped back and let them check her over.

Relief flooded his mind, heart and soul. *Thank You, God*, he muttered under his breath. He would be forever thankful.

"Sir." One of the technicians addressed him. "Looks like we need to check you out, as well."

Ronin had forgotten about his wound.

"Okay, but I'm riding with her."

He followed along beside her as they loaded her in the back of the ambulance. If Thea would have him, he'd never leave her side again.

SIXTEEN

It had been days since they'd released her from the hospital. Four long days that had flown by in a flurry of change. She'd been returned to Portase and taken to the royal vacation home, where she would stay until the changes in the government were complete. Through it all, she hadn't seen a trace of Ronin.

Thea paced the elegant room where she was to meet her visitor. She was home, but it didn't feel like home without Ronin. Doubts filled her mind. Maybe she'd imagined him saying those words.

She couldn't be sure. She had been in shock, they told her. She'd had a severe allergic reaction to some peanut oil Lucia had slipped in her drink and would have died. Lucia was in custody, though; that gave her some peace of mind. Her son, Daniel, had been brought in for questioning, but an in-depth interrogation and further investigation into Lucia's past had proved his innocence. He was just as shocked by what his mother had done as everyone else. He had even agreed to help them in any way possible to locate her sister.

It turned out he had been the man at the event they'd lured her to her first night in Denver. No one really had any idea why Lucia had instructed the men who worked for her in the Royal Guard to direct Thea there. Lucia's reasons for doing what she'd done might be questionable, but she had been very calculating in doing it. She'd been patient in her plan. She'd probably meant to kill her and enjoy the party afterward. If her son hadn't shown up, she'd have pulled it off.

How one person could be so callous of human life, Thea had no idea. At least the woman had a motherly instinct in protecting her child. But it was not her place to make judgment or cast stones. Thea only hoped that whatever happened to the woman, she would never have to see Lucia again.

After learning the full story, Thea could vaguely remember the woman from before her father's death. But her father had been very careful about the sorts of people he allowed around his children. He had been a wise man and had probably sensed Lucia's true nature early on.

Thea did wonder about the things the woman had said, though. She'd mentioned her sister. She could have been just trying to think up new ways to cause Thea pain or it could have been the shock, but Thea couldn't help but wonder. Everyone had thought her dead. What if her sister had been saved, too, but no one knew? Could it be true that Lucia had taken Adriana away and raised her? It didn't seem possible, but then very little of the past week really seemed all that possible. She wouldn't rest until she knew for sure. She had already asked Jarrod if he would see if there were any truths to the things the woman had said. She trusted he would get to the bottom of it all. That meant dredging up more of the past, but she'd dealt with the past a lot since she'd met Ronin.

Something about him had given her the courage to finally face it.

Everything that had happened to her the past few weeks held some thread to the events all those years ago. It was almost as if she'd come full circle. That was the way life worked sometimes.

Thea smiled to herself. She did look forward to parts of the past—her expected guest, for one. She couldn't wait to thank him and apologize on behalf of their country for the hardships that had befallen him after his part in her rescue. She couldn't imagine anything would even begin to make up for it all, but she would do what she could.

She had hoped Ronin would be here. She meant it as a surprise for him more than anything. But she couldn't postpone it forever while she waited and wondered what had happened to him and why he had pulled his latest disappearing act. Everyone who should have known where he was had given her the runaround, as if he was on some top secret mission.

They seemed to forget who they were dealing with. She was their ruler, after all. At least she was for now. Soon, Leo would be here and he could take the spot of head of their government. It was her duty to her country, but a position she didn't want. The past few days had shown her that.

The short amount of time she'd lived in this palace of a home was more than enough to show her it was not a life she wanted. Royalty might be something that was in her bloodline, but it wasn't in her heart. Her dream was cozy evening meals and discussing the day, not discussing politics. S'mores in front of the fire, not waiters serving food she didn't even know the name of.

She wanted a lifetime of snowball fights and puppies. Hopefully, that life would include children with freckles and days of mud pies and doll tea parties. Maybe it was selfish of her to not want what her ancestors before her had fought so hard for her to have. She wasn't sure. She only knew what would make her happy. That had to count for something. She knew a huge part of Ronin's worries had been because of her status. There had to be a way they could work it out so she could do her duty as a member of the royal family and still have a family of her own.

Thea was pulled from her contemplation by a knock at the door.

"Your Highness," the portly man at the door announced. "He's here."

"Thank you. Please show him in."

Thea braced herself for the shock she was certain would come. When the man she'd only seen in dreams became a real, live human, she was sure there would be a moment of surprise. He stepped through the door and she recognized him immediately. Not from her memories—they were still so vague and splotchy it was impossible to know how much of them were real—but because he reminded her so much of his son. He was very much an older version of the man she loved.

"Your Highness," he greeted her as he stepped into the room.

"Please." Thea stood frozen in place. "Please call me Thea." She wasn't sure what was proper or expected, so she did what she felt she needed to do. In a few large strides she reached him and wrapped her arms around him in a hug. "I have so much to thank you for."

"I think it is I who must thank you."

"Pssh," she exhaled. "You saved me first. I'm only repaying the favor." She released him and stepped back. He was clearly taken off guard by her openness. She didn't care. No matter what she did for this man, she could never thank him enough. He had rescued her. He had given up his freedom for her for years without ever risking her safety, and most of all, he had given her Ronin.

"Would you like to sit?" Thea motioned toward a Victorian love seat in the center of the room.

He nodded and took a seat. Thea sat beside him.

"I had hoped to surprise your sons with your visit as well, but they are not here yet. Jarrod and Declan will both be here in a few days and Ronin has taken off somewhere."

"He does that." Calvin Parrish smiled, small dimples playing at his cheeks, reminding her even more of Ronin. "I'm honored that you invited me to spend some time here to see my boys."

"You have amazing sons." She hadn't met Declan yet, but she was sure he'd be honorable like his brothers. "Ronin saved me, you know, just like you did." Thea wasn't sure if *saved* was the right word. Ronin had done so much more. He had helped her face her fears. He had stuck by her even when she'd pushed him away. Of course, he'd done his share of pushing as well, but they both had things they'd had to let go of in order to move forward.

He had said he loved her. Or she thought he had. She still wasn't sure.

"I want you to know, I plan to marry him."

The man choked. She'd caught him off guard again. If Ronin were here he'd tell her how she clearly needed to work more on her tactfulness.

She had to speak her mind, though. Holding back secrets had a way of eating at a person, of giving fear a foothold in their heart. She would never be that person again. For so long fear had had its hold on her. She'd struggled with it, doubting the strength of her own faith because of that struggle. Then she had realized she was only human. It would be a part of her life, but she didn't have to let it control her.

"Not immediately, of course," she added.

She had to convince him first. But she was hoping he wouldn't take much persuading. She hoped that the words he'd spoken the night she'd almost died were heartfelt and still as true now as they'd been then.

"Of course." Calvin smiled.

"You are his father, so I'm sure you already know, but Ronin is an amazing man. I have grown to care for him quite a bit."

A noise at the door distracted her and she looked up.

Ronin stood at the doorway, a small black-and-white puppy wriggling in his arms.

He hadn't meant to eavesdrop, but when he'd heard the voice, he'd recognized it immediately. Thea would forever surprise him, he had no doubt. She'd had his father released and brought here. It only made him love her more. If that were even possible.

Their eyes met and he knew a moment of complete clarity. He'd known before, even if he wasn't sure he had finally begun to believe it. Maybe he'd known since that first night when she'd smacked him with the brick. It had knocked something loose in him, he imagined.

His father turned, following Thea's gaze toward the door.

"Ronin." He smiled and rose to greet his son.

"Dad." Ronin shifted the puppy to one side to return his father's hug. He held on tight. He'd spent so many years dreaming of the day he'd see his father free and Thea had made it happen. He searched his mind for the words, but none could fully express his joy at seeing him freed. "It's so good to see you. Have you been here long?" His mind raced with questions. Had Thea been planning this all along?

"I just got here."

"I had hoped to surprise you," Thea whispered.

"You did. I wasn't expecting it at all." He'd known his father would be released. There was no doubt in his mind. Now that the real person behind the king's death and the recent threats had been found and put away, they'd have no reason to hold him.

He felt a small twinge of guilt that his father's release hadn't been in the forefront of his mind. When he'd gone to find the prince and princess, he'd had one goal in mind—proving his father's innocence and restoring honor to his family.

Somewhere along the way his focus had shifted. He hadn't even realized it until he'd nearly lost her. In the days before the attack on Thea's life, his main objective had been her.

Her faith and love had chased away the bitterness over what had happened. He hadn't even realized how much it had consumed him. Now he could look back and see how she'd shown him the importance of letting go of the past. Holding on to it and letting vengeance guide you would lead a person down a bitter path to loneliness and pain.

He'd been on that path.

But not anymore. Thea's faith and love had changed him. She made him want to be a better man. She gave him the strength to believe in things he'd given up on a long time ago.

"It's been a long trip. If you don't mind, Princess Dorthea, I could use a few hours to rest up," his father said.

Thea glared at the man, that same glare she'd used on him when he'd called her by her given name.

"She goes by Thea now, Dad." He smiled. His father had rescued her as a young teen. She'd been on the path to a life of royalty. Then Ronin had rescued her as a woman who had lived a life of hiding and fear. Together they'd learned to trust and to love.

"So she does, son. So she does." His father clasped his hand before leaving the room and leaned over to whisper in his ear, "Don't mess this up." He winked and then was gone.

Ronin had no plans of messing anything up, not any more than he had already anyway.

"Where have you been?" Thea questioned when they were alone. "I looked all over for you. I wanted to surprise you with your father's visit."

"I am surprised." Ronin shifted the puppy again as it squirmed to get down on the floor and run around. It had been his intention to never leave her side again, but he'd had a few things he really wanted to take care of first. "I'm sorry if I made you worry."

"I was worried." Thea chewed her bottom lip and looked between him and the puppy. "I thought you might have changed your mind and left me again."

"Changed my mind about what?"

He had a good idea what she was thinking, but he wanted to know how much she remembered of the night she'd almost died.

"It doesn't matter." She shook her head and moved toward him, her hand reaching out to stroke the puppy's fur. "I see you've made a new friend."

"Don't you recognize her?"

Thea glanced from the puppy to his face and back to the puppy. Her eyes filled with surprise, joy and, if he wasn't mistaken, a light sheen of tears.

"I thought maybe, but…"

"But what?" he asked.

"Can I hold her?"

"Of course. She's for you."

"For me?" Thea gasped. Ronin noticed a tiny tear make its way down her cheek as she grabbed the puppy. She cuddled it in her arms, then turned away quickly, wiping at her face.

"But what, Thea?" he asked again, encouraging her to open up and share with him. He wouldn't blame her if she didn't. The last time she'd shared her feelings, it hadn't gone so well.

He would do better this time. He knew now what she'd been trying to tell him that day. When love happened, it wasn't something that took months or years to know. You just knew.

And he did know now.

"But it's just too amazing to be true, I guess." She spoke in a whisper. "That you would go all the way back to Kansas to pick up a puppy for me."

"I would go all the way to the moon and back for you," he answered, hoping his words conveyed the deepness of the emotion he felt for her.

"Is that so?" She turned to face him.

He nodded and stepped toward her. "I was a fool and I hurt you. I'm sorry for that."

He was so very sorry. He hoped she would

give him the rest of their lives to show her just how much he regretted causing her any pain.

"That night when you said you…" Her voice trailed off in a whisper. He couldn't blame her for not wanting to say it, to risk the rejection again. The puppy wiggled against her and she hugged it close to her heart.

"That night I realized for a few moments what my life would be like without you. I didn't like what I saw." Ronin reached out to her and lifted her chin with his fingers. He wanted to look into her eyes as he confessed his love. "You have shown me what love is, what love can be. Without you I'd have ended up a bitter, lonely man."

"And with me?" She smiled, her face mirroring the same love he felt.

"With you I have everything." He wrapped his arms around her and pulled her close. The puppy wiggled between them. "I was worried I couldn't handle you being a princess. I thought I would end up being the little man behind the woman. But what does that matter? Without you I have nothing."

"You will never be a little man." Thea bent over and placed the puppy on the floor. It ran circles around their feet, tugging at the leg of his pants. Thea returned to his arms and he held her close.

"But you will forever be my princess." Ronin bent his head, slowly bringing his lips to hers in a soft kiss. It was everything he thought it would be and more. "Whether you are ruling your kingdom from the throne or being the queen of a farmhouse filled with puppies and children, you are the princess of my heart."

She looked at him, her eyes filled with love and hope. She reached up and softly ran her fingers over his cheek. "I do love you so," she said softly.

The puppy yipped at their feet for attention, but Ronin was reluctant to let Thea out of his arms. This was their beginning. He was surprised it had taken him so long to realize how much holding her felt like home. Now that he had her, he was never letting her go.

He had rescued her. But really, she had rescued him.

She smiled up at him, and he saw that look that he had come to admire so much.

"But this is the way it's going to be," she teased, using his own words against him. A smile spread across her face and lit her eyes with infectious joy.

"Oh, it is, is it?" Ronin laughed.

He couldn't wait to hear what she had to say because he knew no matter what outlandish idea she followed that statement up with, he would gladly go along with it. She was, after all, his princess.

* * * * *

Dear Reader,

Thank you so much for reading my first book, *Royal Rescue*. Publication with Harlequin has for many, many years been a dream of mine. I was thrilled and honored to have my dream come true through "The Search for a Killer Voice" pitch event.

When I first started writing the story of Thea and Ronin, Psalms 91:4 was in my heart and mind.

He will cover you with His feathers and under His wings you will find refuge.

Thea had for so long been alone and frightened of a past she could barely remember. Like so many of us, she had lost pieces of herself along the way and nearly forgotten who she really was. Despite her struggles, she remained strong in her faith and knew her true refuge could be found in God. As the story progressed and Thea and Ronin's relationship grew, I began to realize the story was more about keeping those parts of us hidden away, being afraid to step out and claim the title that is rightfully ours. It was then I realized what I really wanted you, the reader, to take away from the story. You need to be confident of who you are in Christ.

We are all Royalty, Daughters and Sons of the Most High King. Hold your head high and never let anyone or anything convince you that you are anything less.

I hope you enjoyed *Royal Rescue* and that my words brought you happiness and in some way fueled your faith. I'd love to hear from readers through my website at www.tammyjohnson.net.

Tammy Johnson

LARGER-PRINT BOOKS!

GET 2 FREE
LARGER-PRINT NOVELS
PLUS 2 FREE
MYSTERY GIFTS

Love Inspired

Larger-print novels are now available...

LILPDIR13R

REQUEST YOUR FREE BOOKS!
2 FREE WHOLESOME ROMANCE NOVELS IN LARGER PRINT
PLUS 2 FREE MYSTERY GIFTS

※※※※※※※※※※※※※※※※※※※※※※※※

HEARTWARMING™

⚜⚜⚜⚜⚜⚜⚜⚜⚜⚜⚜⚜⚜⚜⚜⚜⚜⚜⚜⚜⚜⚜⚜

Wholesome, tender romances

YES! Please send me 2 FREE Harlequin® Heartwarming Larger-Print novels and my 2 FREE mystery gifts (gifts worth about $10). After receiving them, if I don't wish to receive any more books, I can return the shipping statement marked "cancel." If I don't cancel, I will receive 4 brand-new larger-print novels every month and be billed just $4.99 per book in the U.S. or $5.74 per book in Canada. That's a savings of at least 23% off the cover price. It's quite a bargain! Shipping and handling is just 50¢ per book in the U.S. and 75¢ per book in Canada.* I understand that accepting the 2 free books and gifts places me under no obligation to buy anything. I can always return a shipment and cancel at any time. Even if I never buy another book, the two free books and gifts are mine to keep forever.

161/361 IDN F47N

Name _____ (PLEASE PRINT) _____

Address _____ Apt. # _____

City _____ State/Prov. _____ Zip/Postal Code _____

Signature (if under 18, a parent or guardian must sign) _____

Mail to the **Harlequin® Reader Service:**
IN U.S.A.: P.O. Box 1867, Buffalo, NY 14240-1867
IN CANADA: P.O. Box 609, Fort Erie, Ontario L2A 5X3

* Terms and prices subject to change without notice. Prices do not include applicable taxes. Sales tax applicable in N.Y. Canadian residents will be charged applicable taxes. Offer not valid in Quebec. This offer is limited to one order per household. Not valid for current subscribers to Harlequin Heartwarming larger-print books. All orders subject to credit approval. Credit or debit balances in a customer's account(s) may be offset by any other outstanding balance owed by or to the customer. Please allow 4 to 6 weeks for delivery. Offer available while quantities last.

Your Privacy—The Harlequin® Reader Service is committed to protecting your privacy. Our Privacy Policy is available online at www.ReaderService.com or upon request from the Harlequin Reader Service.

We make a portion of our mailing list available to reputable third parties that offer products we believe may interest you. If you prefer that we not exchange your name with third parties, or if you wish to clarify or modify your communication preferences, please visit us at www.ReaderService.com/consumerchoice or write to us at Harlequin Reader Service Preference Service, P.O. Box 9062, Buffalo, NY 14269. Include your complete name and address.

HWDIR13R